Disney

DESCENDANTS

THE ROTTEN TO THE CORE TRILOGY

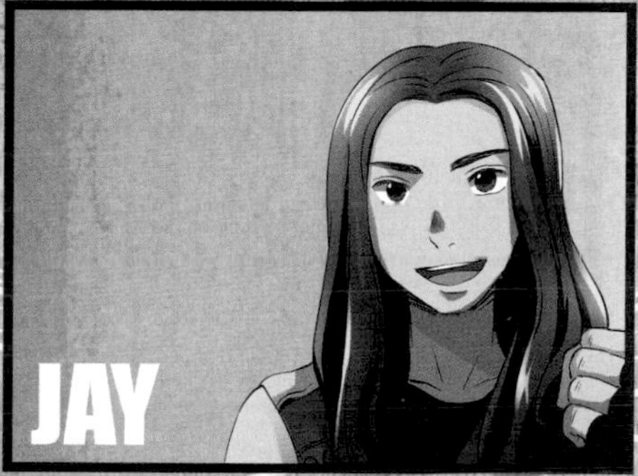
JAY
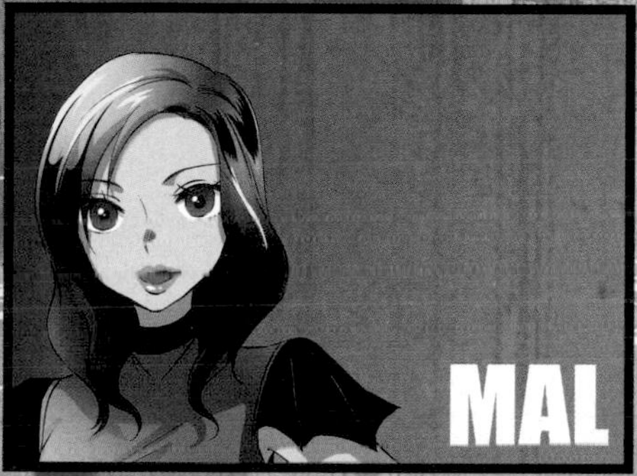
MAL
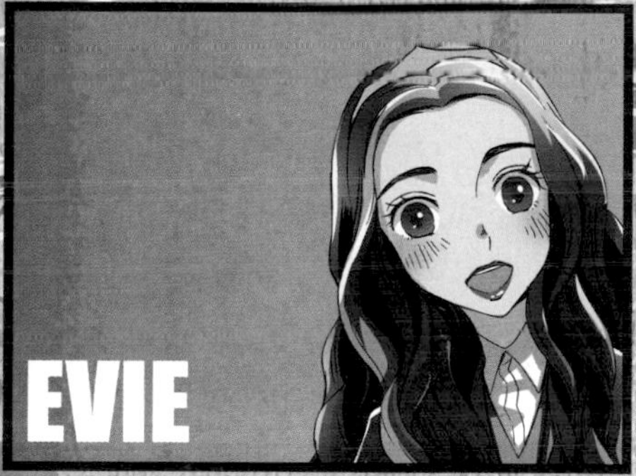
EVIE
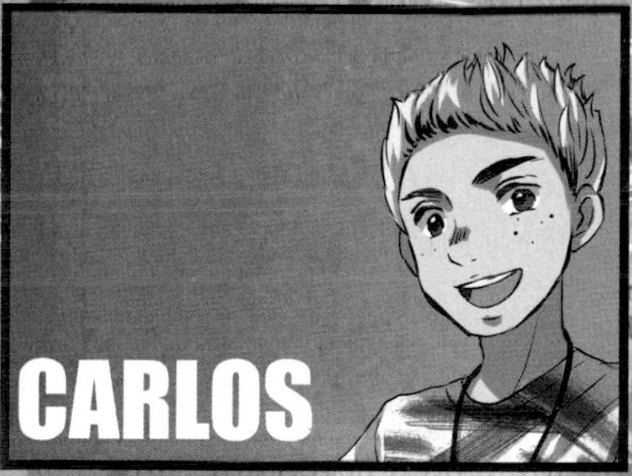
CARLOS

ADAPTED BY: JASON MUELL
ART BY: NATSUKI MINAMI

TOKYOPOP®

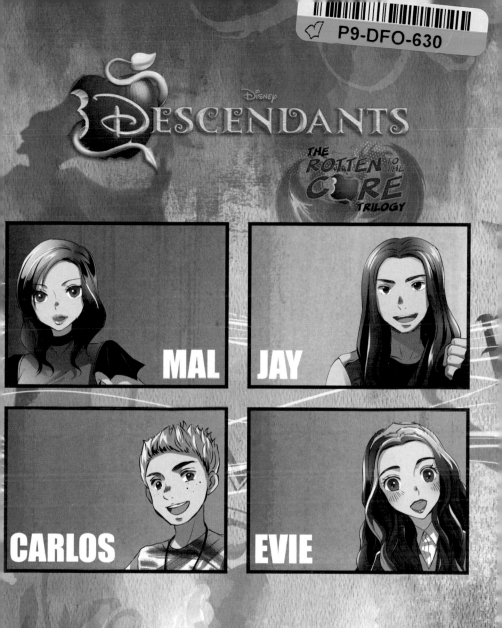

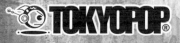

THE STORY SO FAR...

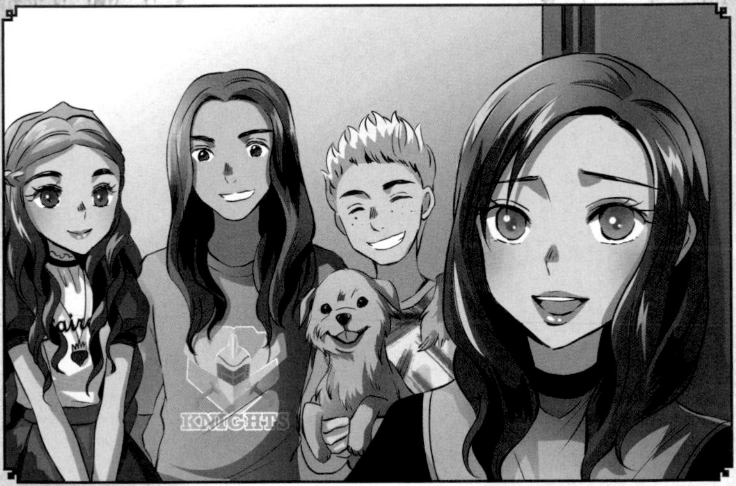
KNIGHTS

The VKs -- Mal, Evie, Jay and Carlos -- had a foolproof evil scheme to get Ben to fall in love with Mal... And it worked!

After Mal's romantic date with Ben, Evie's unexpected academic success, Jay's winning team spirit, and Carlos' bonding with Dude, the VKs are experiencing the best of what Auradon Prep has to offer!

Will they still go through with their plans to destroy all that is good? Follow along as the VKs make some of the biggest decisions of their lives... for better or for worse.

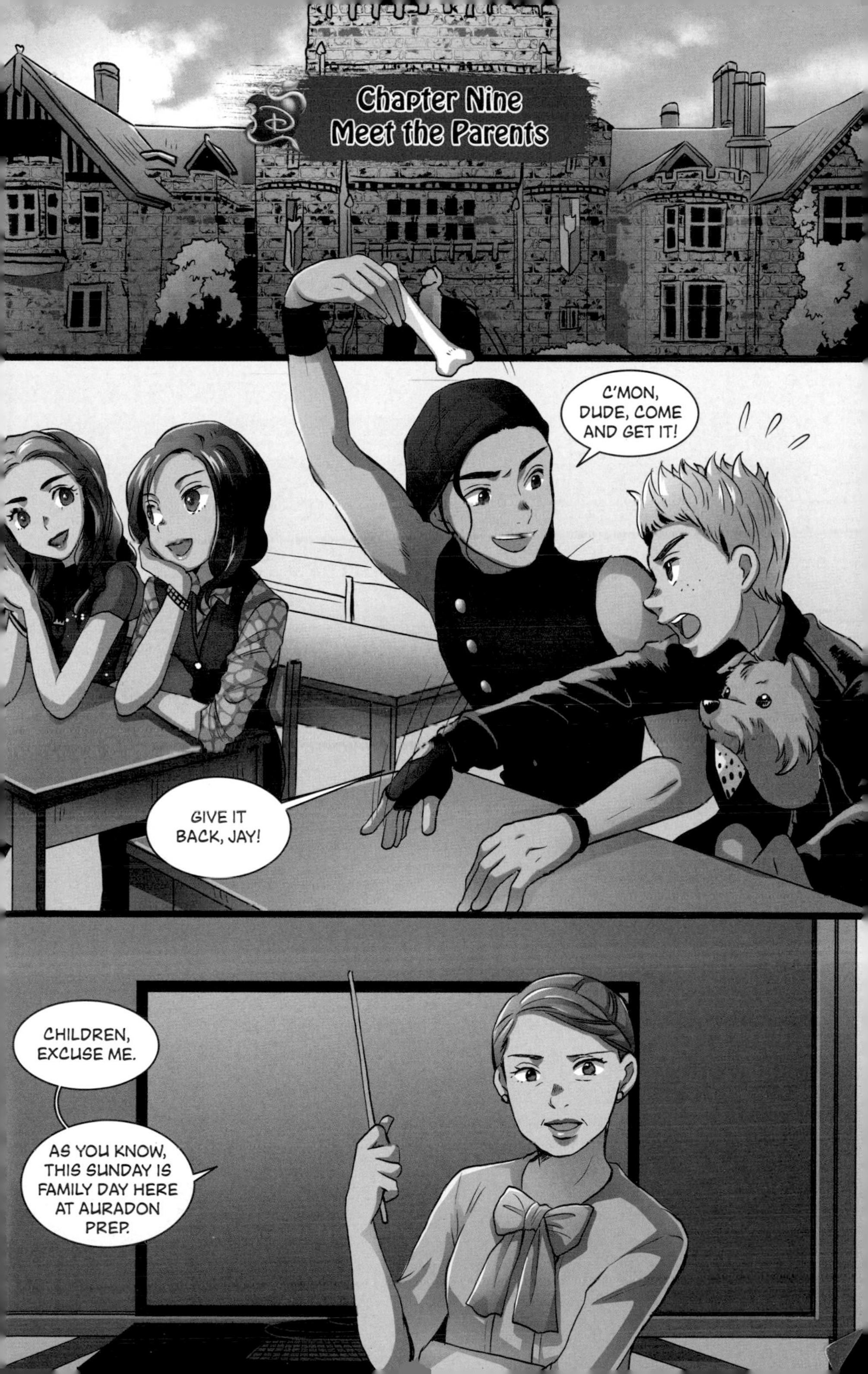
Chapter Nine
Meet the Parents
C'MON, DUDE, COME AND GET IT!
GIVE IT BACK, JAY!
CHILDREN, EXCUSE ME.
AS YOU KNOW, THIS SUNDAY IS FAMILY DAY HERE AT AURADON PREP.

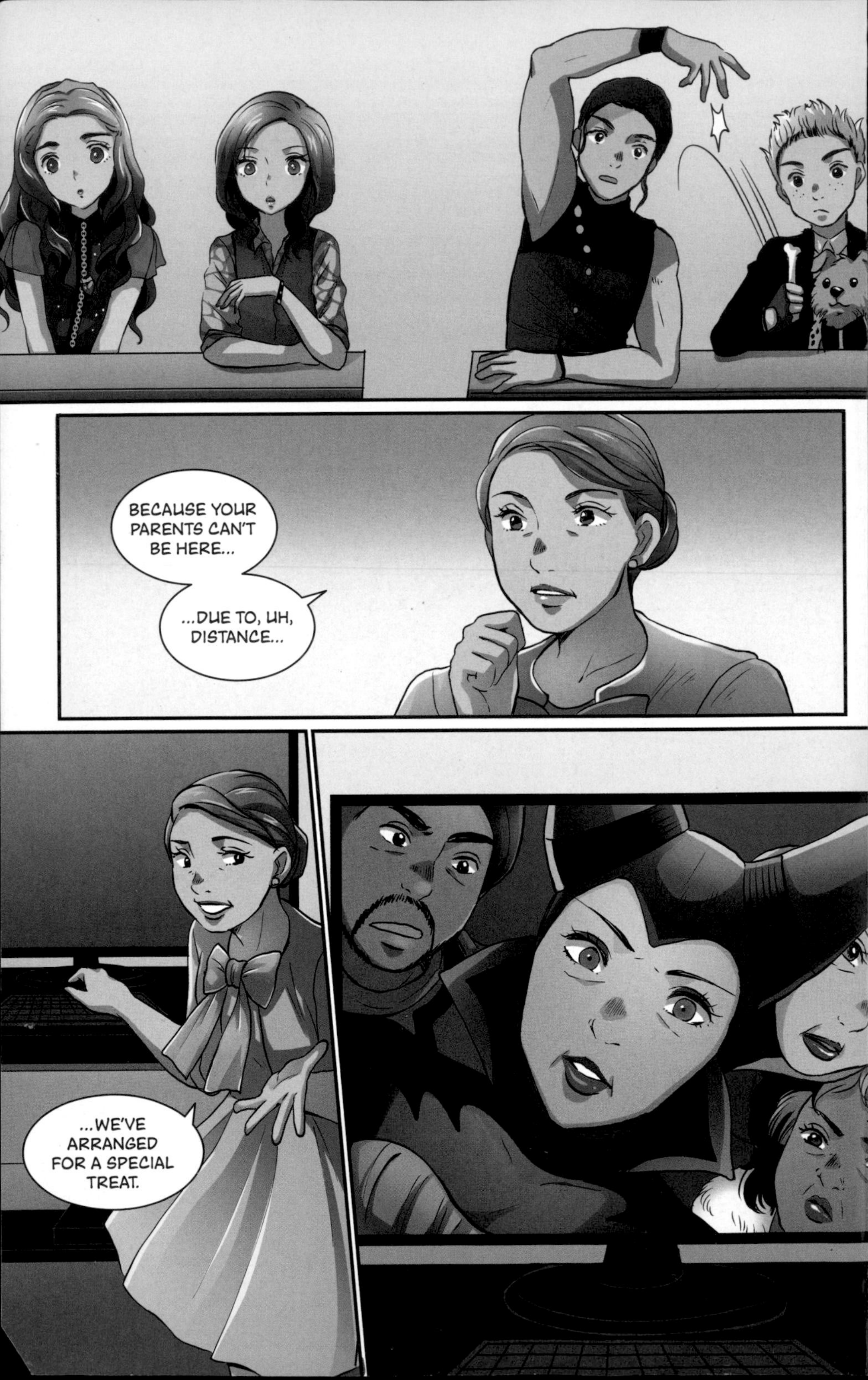
BECAUSE YOUR PARENTS CAN'T BE HERE...
...DUE TO, UH, DISTANCE...
...WE'VE ARRANGED FOR A SPECIAL TREAT.

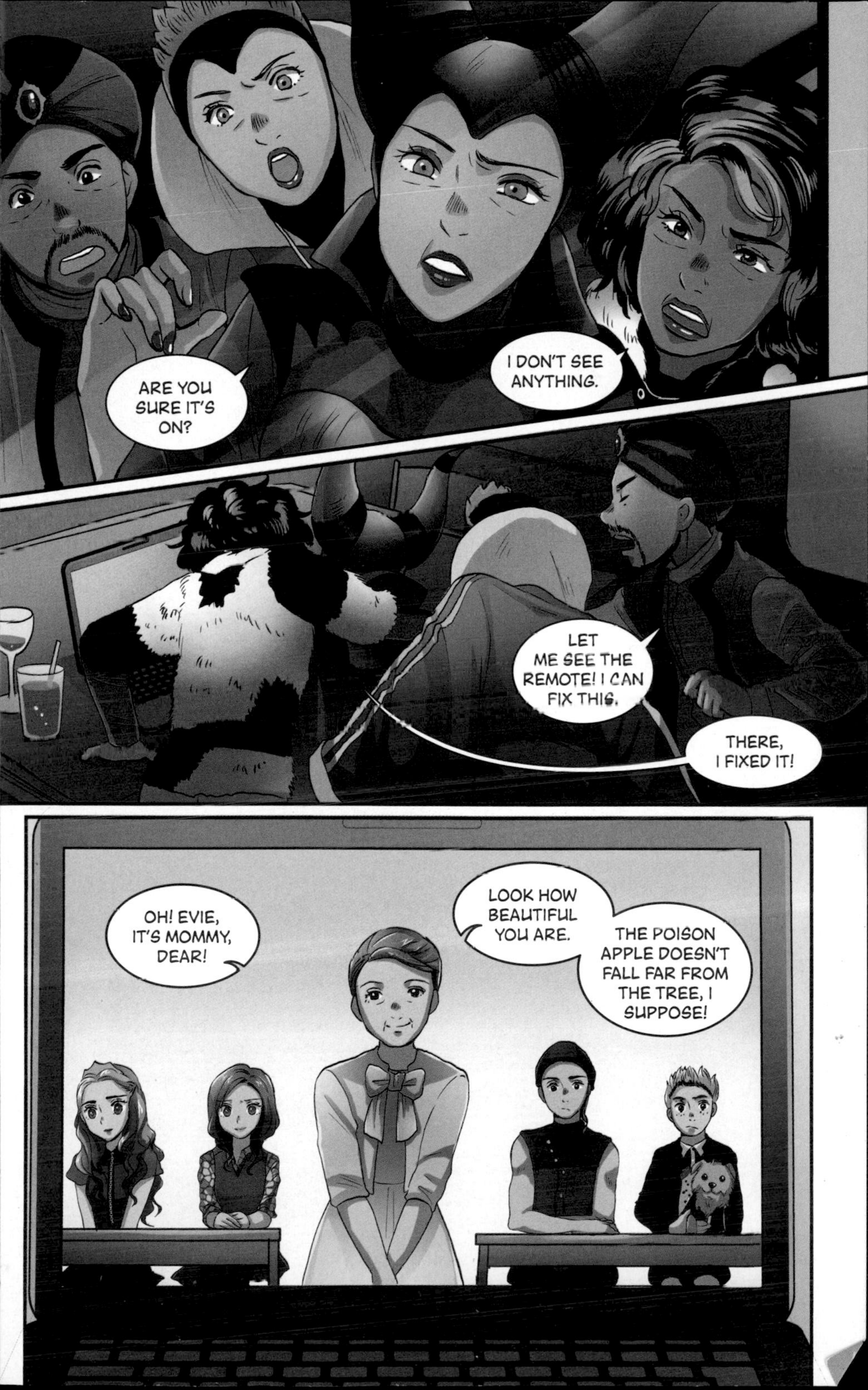
ARE YOU SURE IT'S ON?
I DON'T SEE ANYTHING.
LET ME SEE THE REMOTE! I CAN FIX THIS.
THERE, I FIXED IT!
OH! EVIE, IT'S MOMMY, DEAR!
LOOK HOW BEAUTIFUL YOU ARE.
THE POISON APPLE DOESN'T FALL FAR FROM THE TREE, I SUPPOSE!

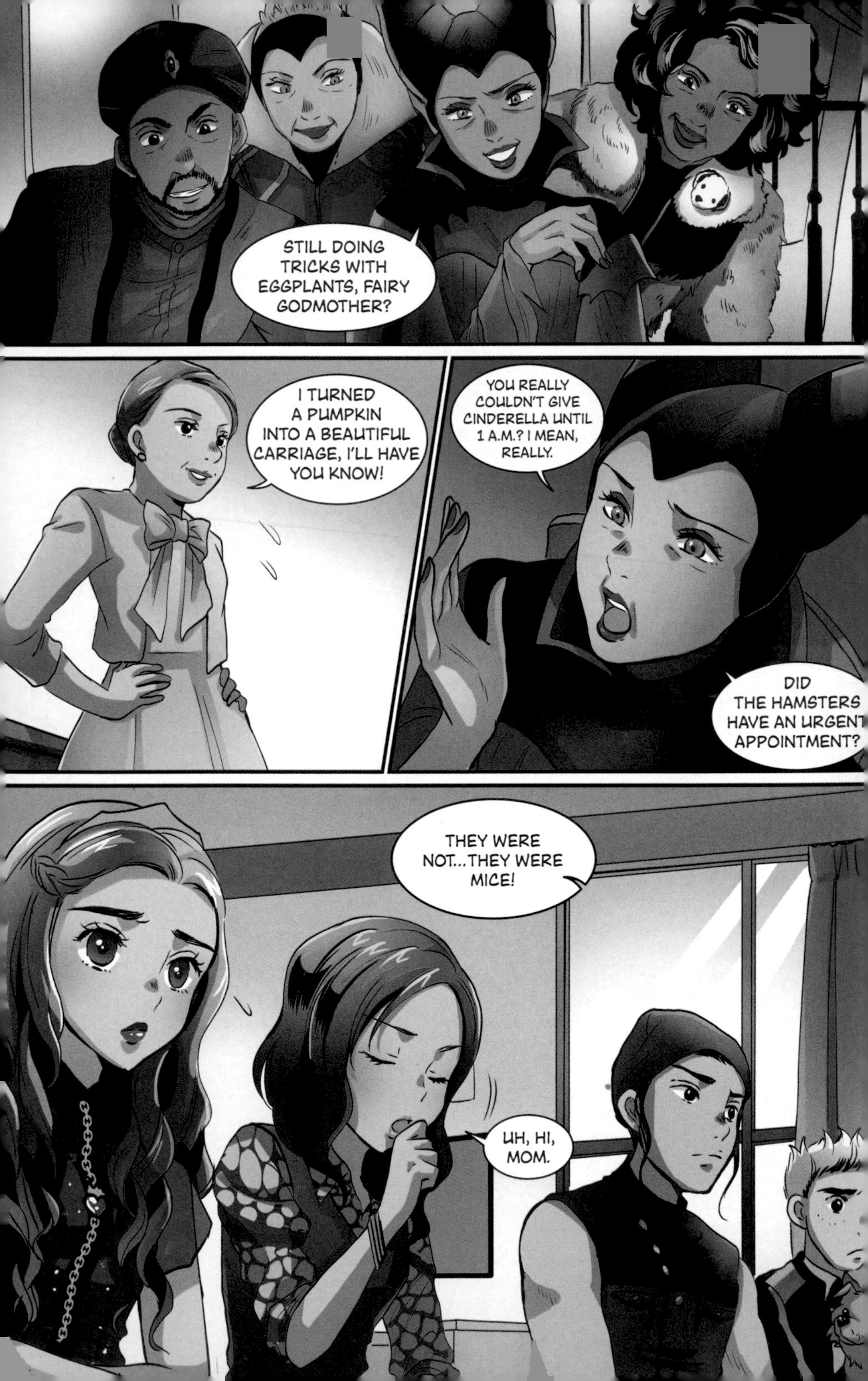
STILL DOING TRICKS WITH EGGPLANTS, FAIRY GODMOTHER?
I TURNED A PUMPKIN INTO A BEAUTIFUL CARRIAGE, I'LL HAVE YOU KNOW!
YOU REALLY COULDN'T GIVE CINDERELLA UNTIL 1 A.M.? I MEAN, REALLY.
DID THE HAMSTERS HAVE AN URGENT APPOINTMENT?
THEY WERE NOT...THEY WERE MICE!
UH, HI, MOM.

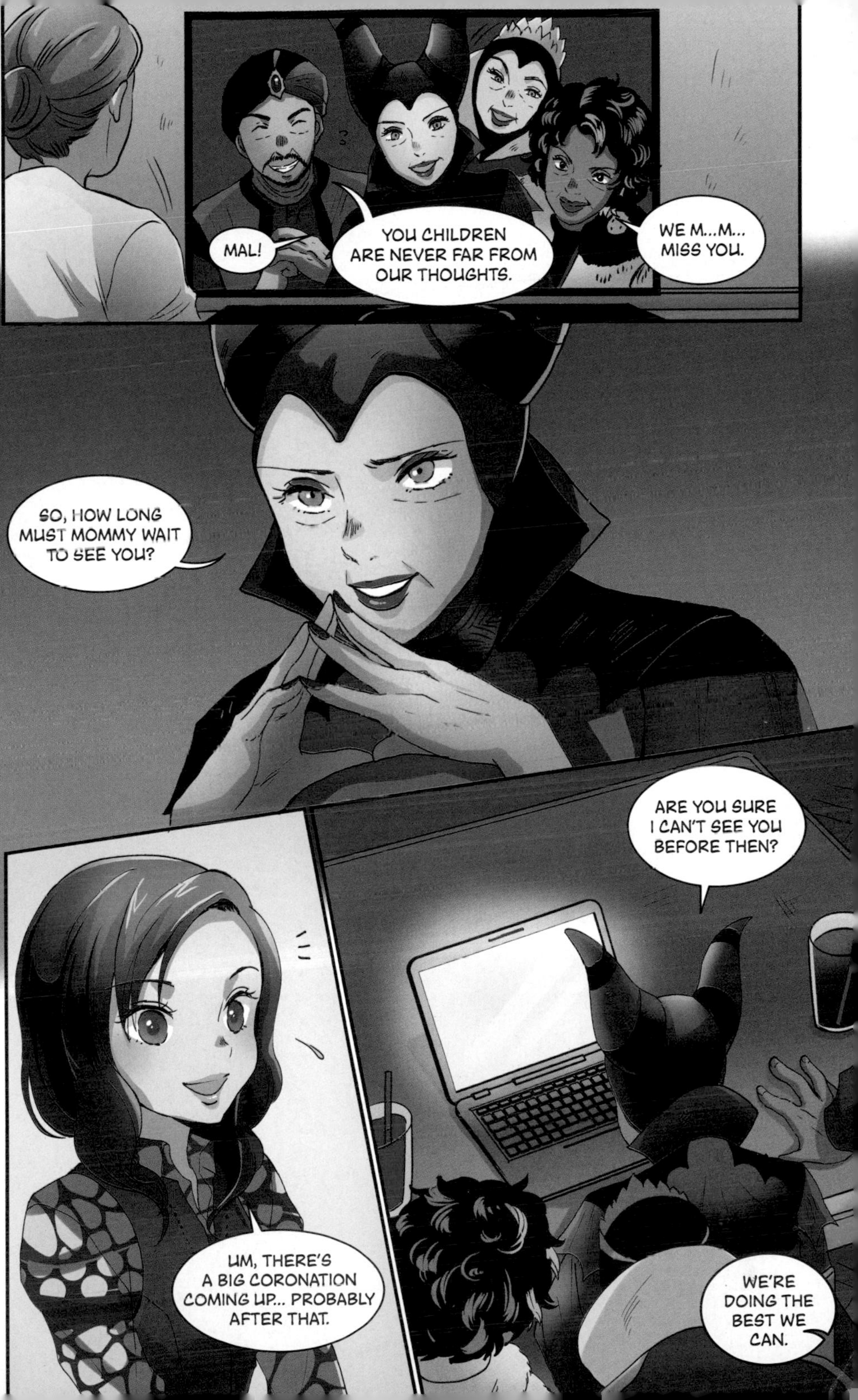
MAL!
YOU CHILDREN ARE NEVER FAR FROM OUR THOUGHTS.
WE M...M... MISS YOU.
SO, HOW LONG MUST MOMMY WAIT TO SEE YOU?
UM, THERE'S A BIG CORONATION COMING UP... PROBABLY AFTER THAT.
ARE YOU SURE I CAN'T SEE YOU BEFORE THEN?
WE'RE DOING THE BEST WE CAN.

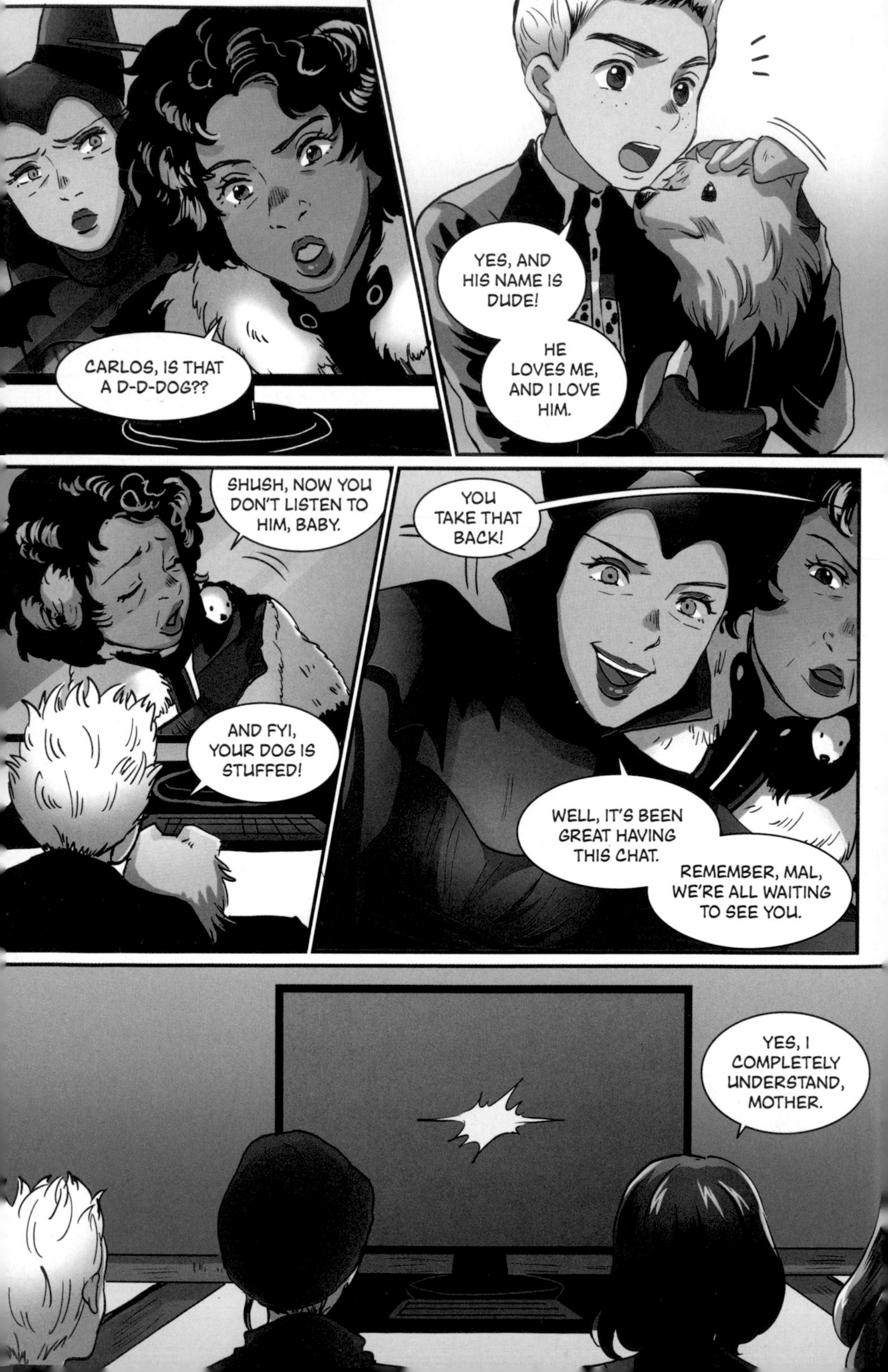
CARLOS, IS THAT A D-D-DOG??
YES, AND HIS NAME IS DUDE!
HE LOVES ME, AND I LOVE HIM.
SHUSH, NOW YOU DON'T LISTEN TO HIM, BABY.
AND FYI, YOUR DOG IS STUFFED!
YOU TAKE THAT BACK!
WELL, IT'S BEEN GREAT HAVING THIS CHAT.
REMEMBER, MAL, WE'RE ALL WAITING TO SEE YOU.
YES, I COMPLETELY UNDERSTAND, MOTHER.

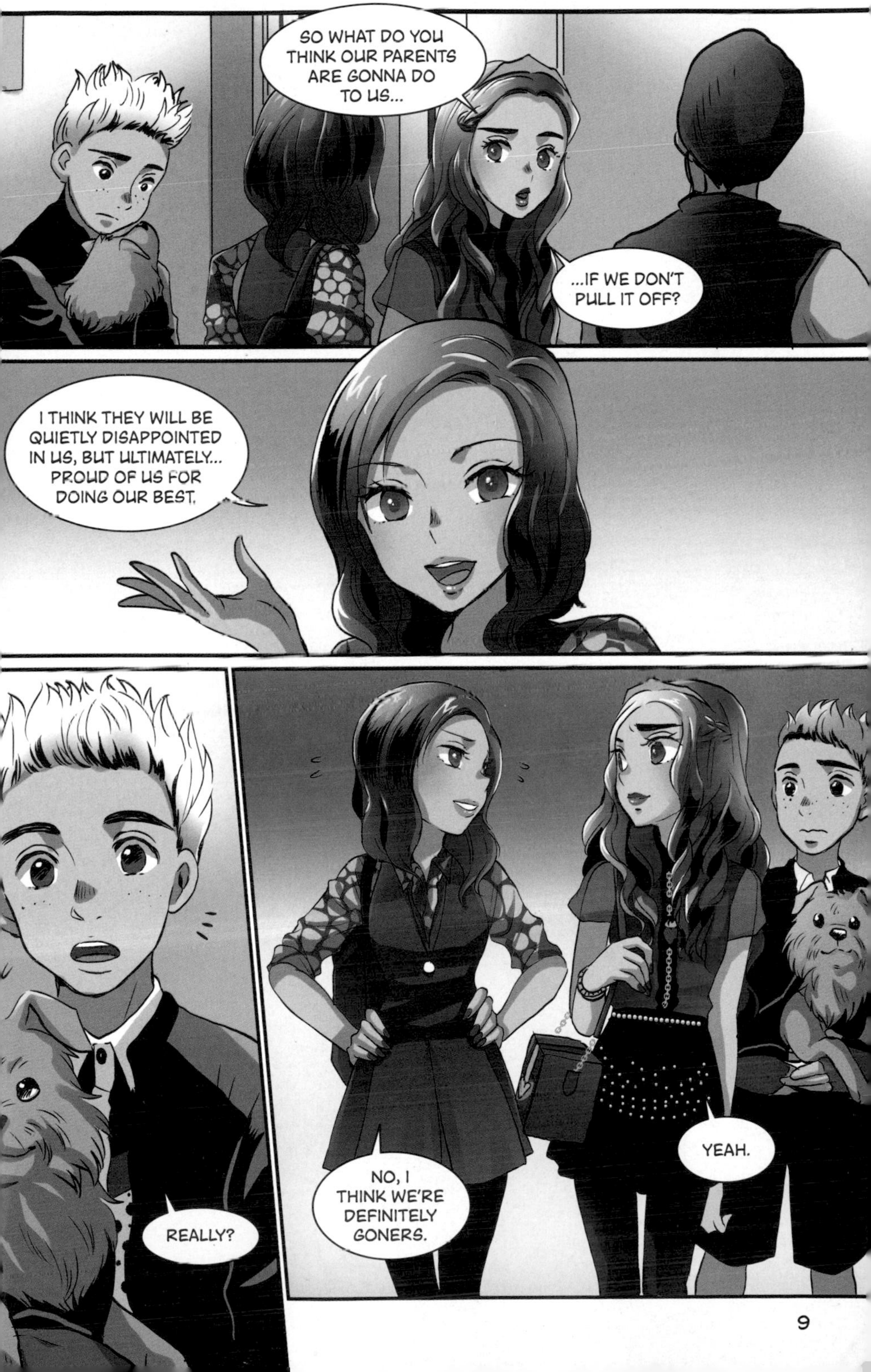
SO WHAT DO YOU THINK OUR PARENTS ARE GONNA DO TO US...
...IF WE DON'T PULL IT OFF?
I THINK THEY WILL BE QUIETLY DISAPPOINTED IN US, BUT ULTIMATELY... PROUD OF US FOR DOING OUR BEST.
REALLY?
NO, I THINK WE'RE DEFINITELY GONERS.
YEAH.

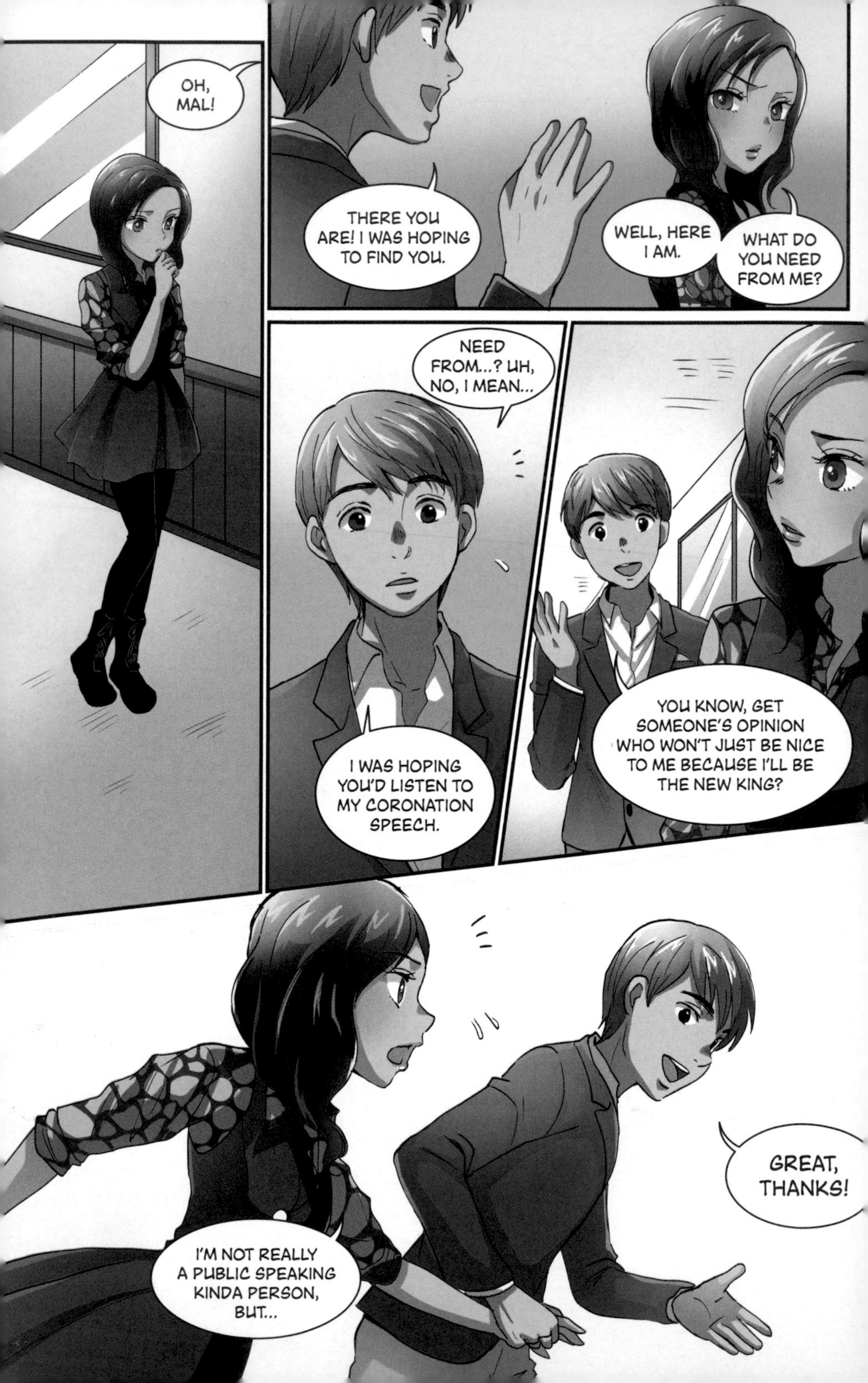

OH, MAL!
THERE YOU ARE! I WAS HOPING TO FIND YOU.
WELL, HERE I AM.
WHAT DO YOU NEED FROM ME?
NEED FROM...? UH, NO, I MEAN...
I WAS HOPING YOU'D LISTEN TO MY CORONATION SPEECH.
YOU KNOW, GET SOMEONE'S OPINION WHO WON'T JUST BE NICE TO ME BECAUSE I'LL BE THE NEW KING?
I'M NOT REALLY A PUBLIC SPEAKING KINDA PERSON, BUT...
GREAT, THANKS!

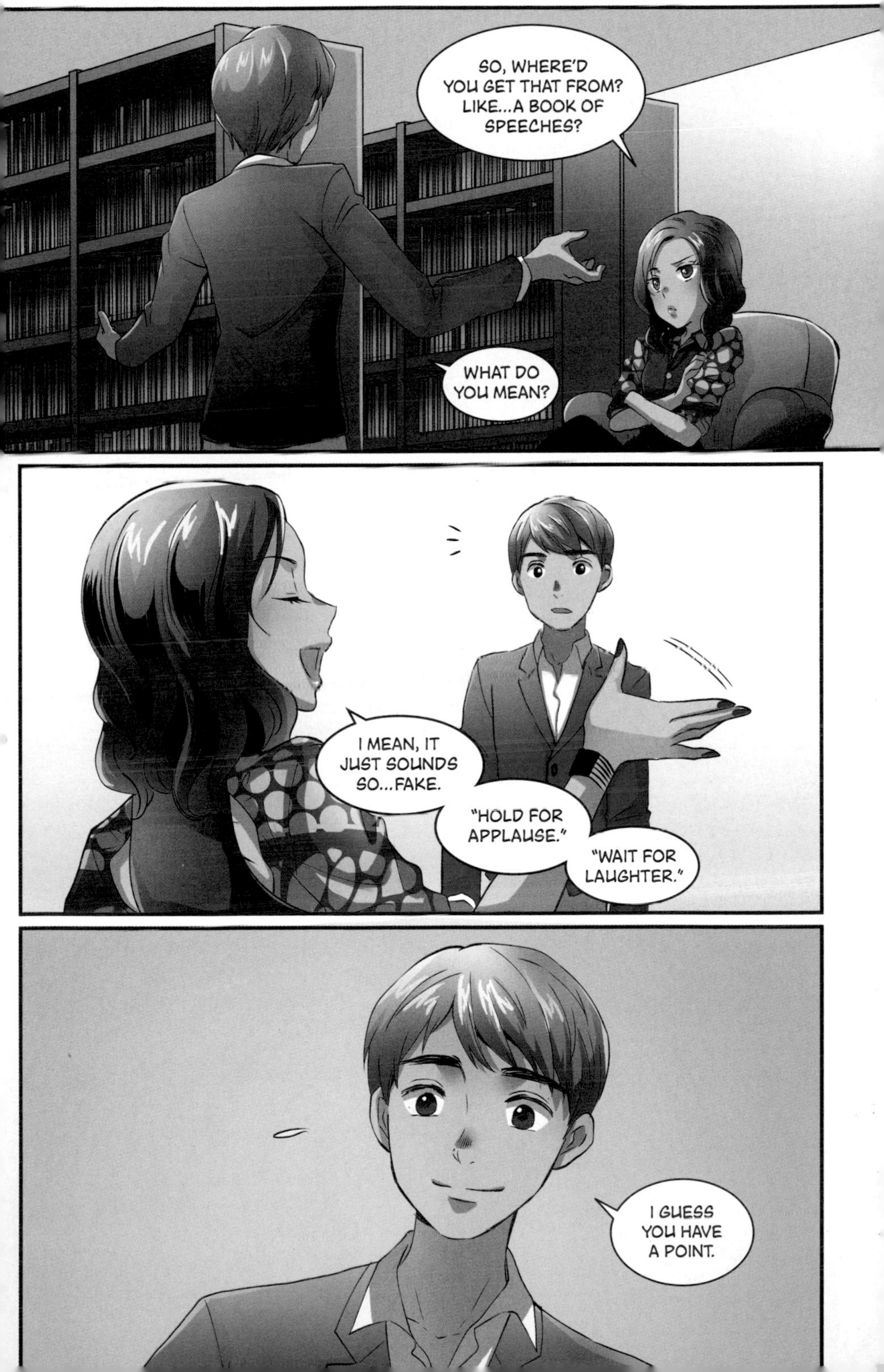
SO, WHERE'D YOU GET THAT FROM? LIKE...A BOOK OF SPEECHES?
WHAT DO YOU MEAN?
I MEAN, IT JUST SOUNDS SO...FAKE.
"HOLD FOR APPLAUSE."
"WAIT FOR LAUGHTER."
I GUESS YOU HAVE A POINT.

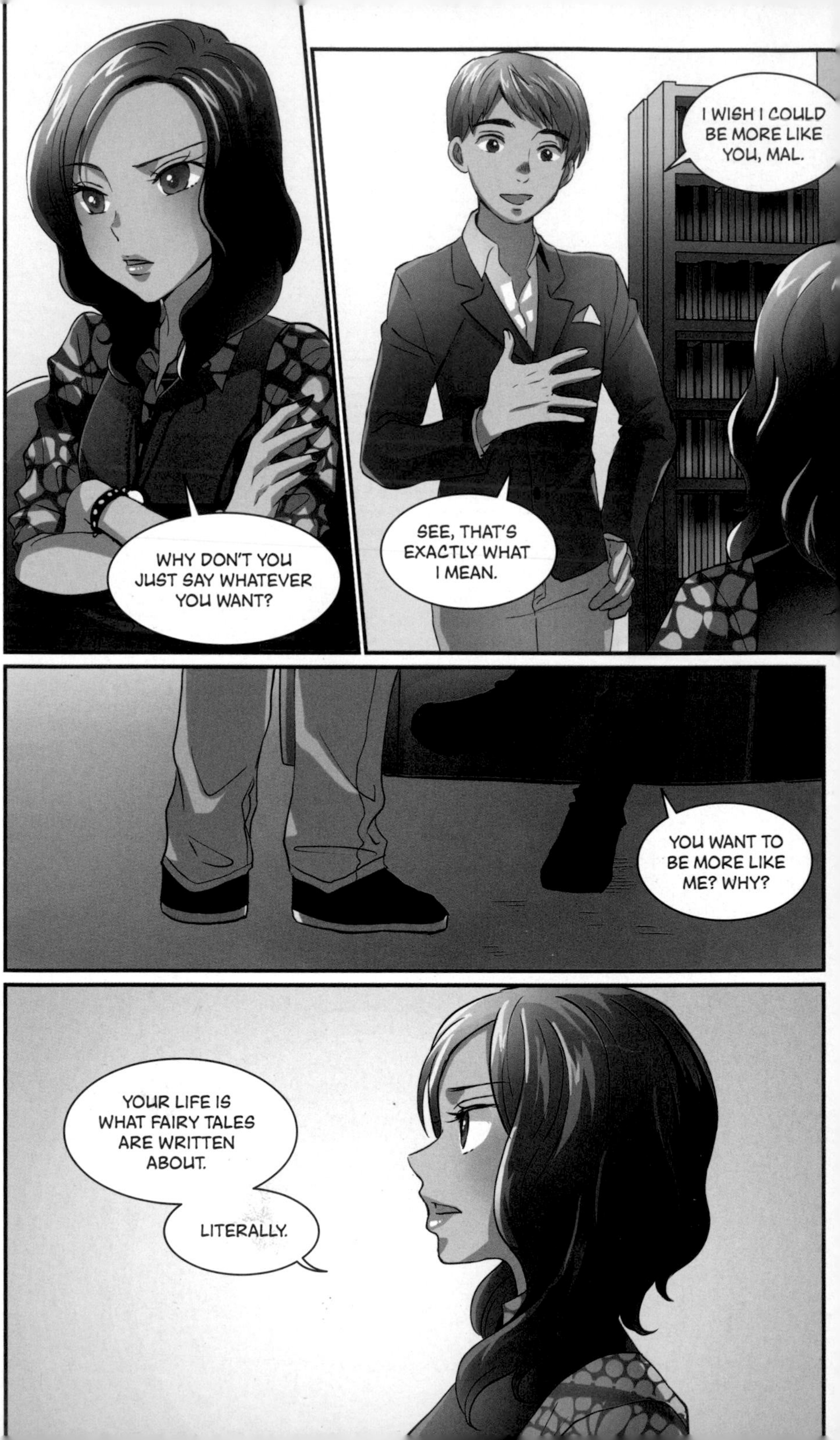
I WISH I COULD BE MORE LIKE YOU, MAL.
WHY DON'T YOU JUST SAY WHATEVER YOU WANT?
SEE, THAT'S EXACTLY WHAT I MEAN.
YOU WANT TO BE MORE LIKE ME? WHY?
YOUR LIFE IS WHAT FAIRY TALES ARE WRITTEN ABOUT.
LITERALLY.

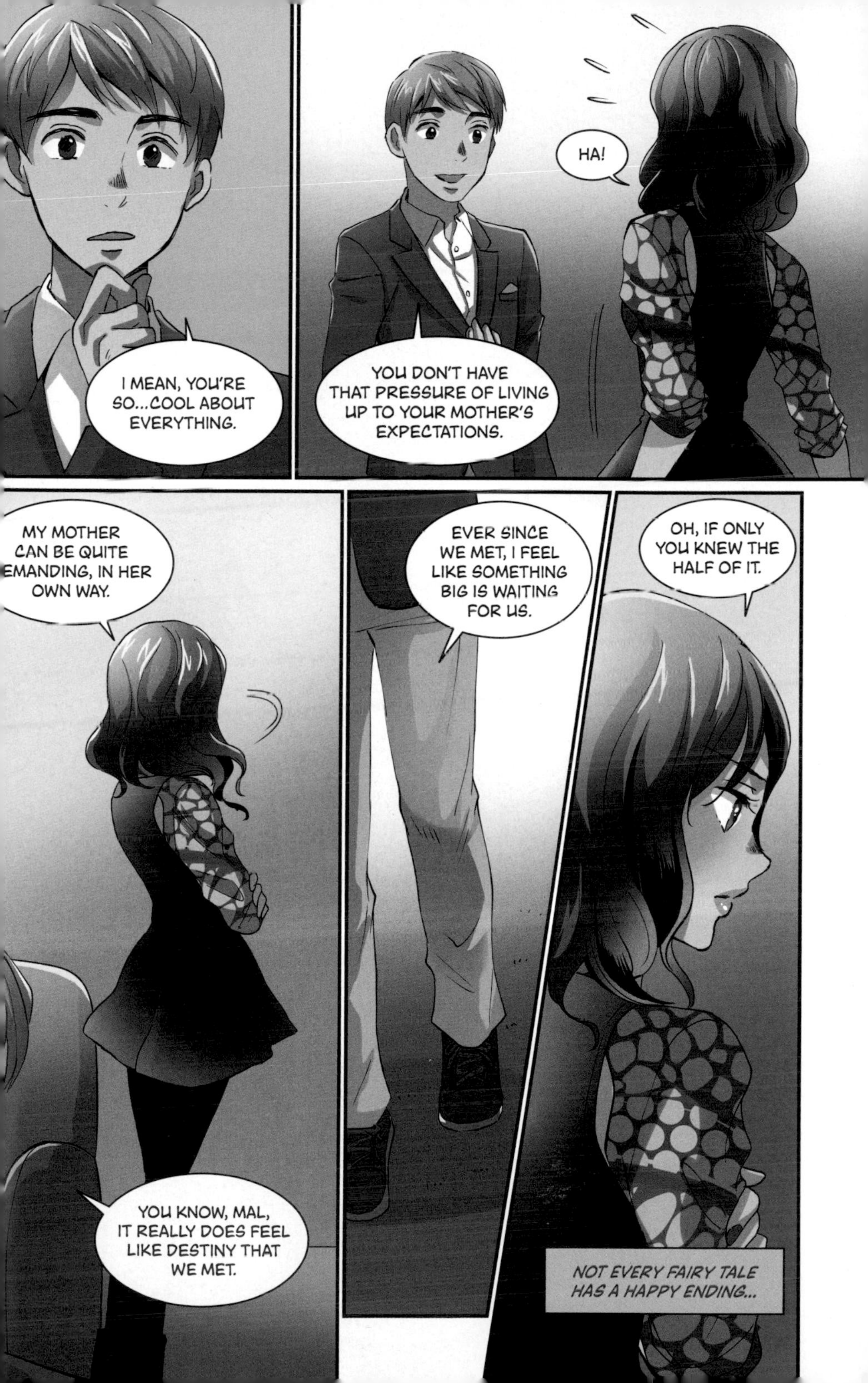
I MEAN, YOU'RE SO...COOL ABOUT EVERYTHING.
YOU DON'T HAVE THAT PRESSURE OF LIVING UP TO YOUR MOTHER'S EXPECTATIONS.
HA!
MY MOTHER CAN BE QUITE EMANDING, IN HER OWN WAY.
YOU KNOW, MAL, IT REALLY DOES FEEL LIKE DESTINY THAT WE MET.
EVER SINCE WE MET, I FEEL LIKE SOMETHING BIG IS WAITING FOR US.
OH, IF ONLY YOU KNEW THE HALF OF IT.
NOT EVERY FAIRY TALE HAS A HAPPY ENDING...

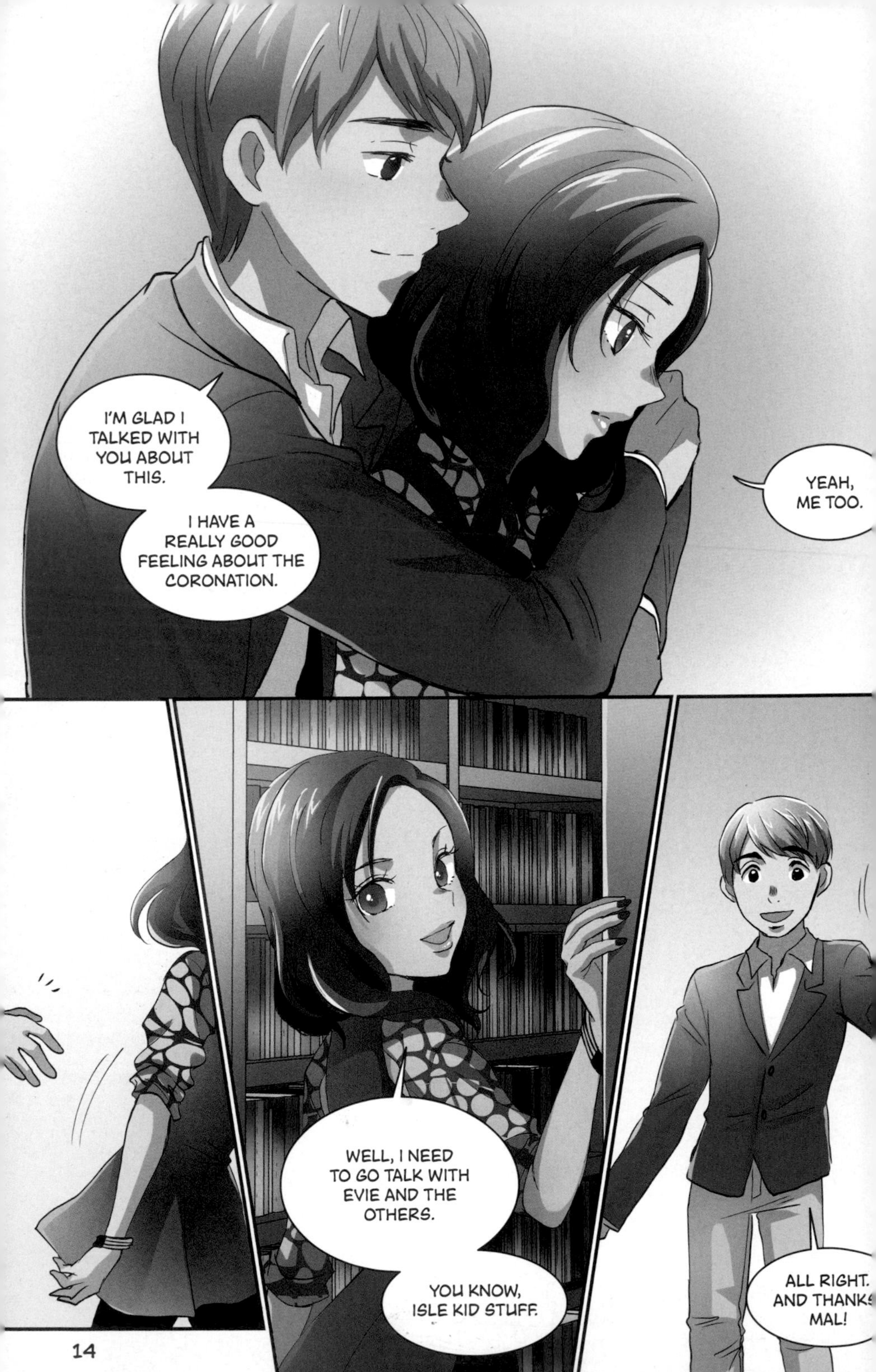
I'M GLAD I TALKED WITH YOU ABOUT THIS.
I HAVE A REALLY GOOD FEELING ABOUT THE CORONATION.
YEAH, ME TOO.
WELL, I NEED TO GO TALK WITH EVIE AND THE OTHERS.
YOU KNOW, ISLE KID STUFF.
ALL RIGHT. AND THANKS MAL!

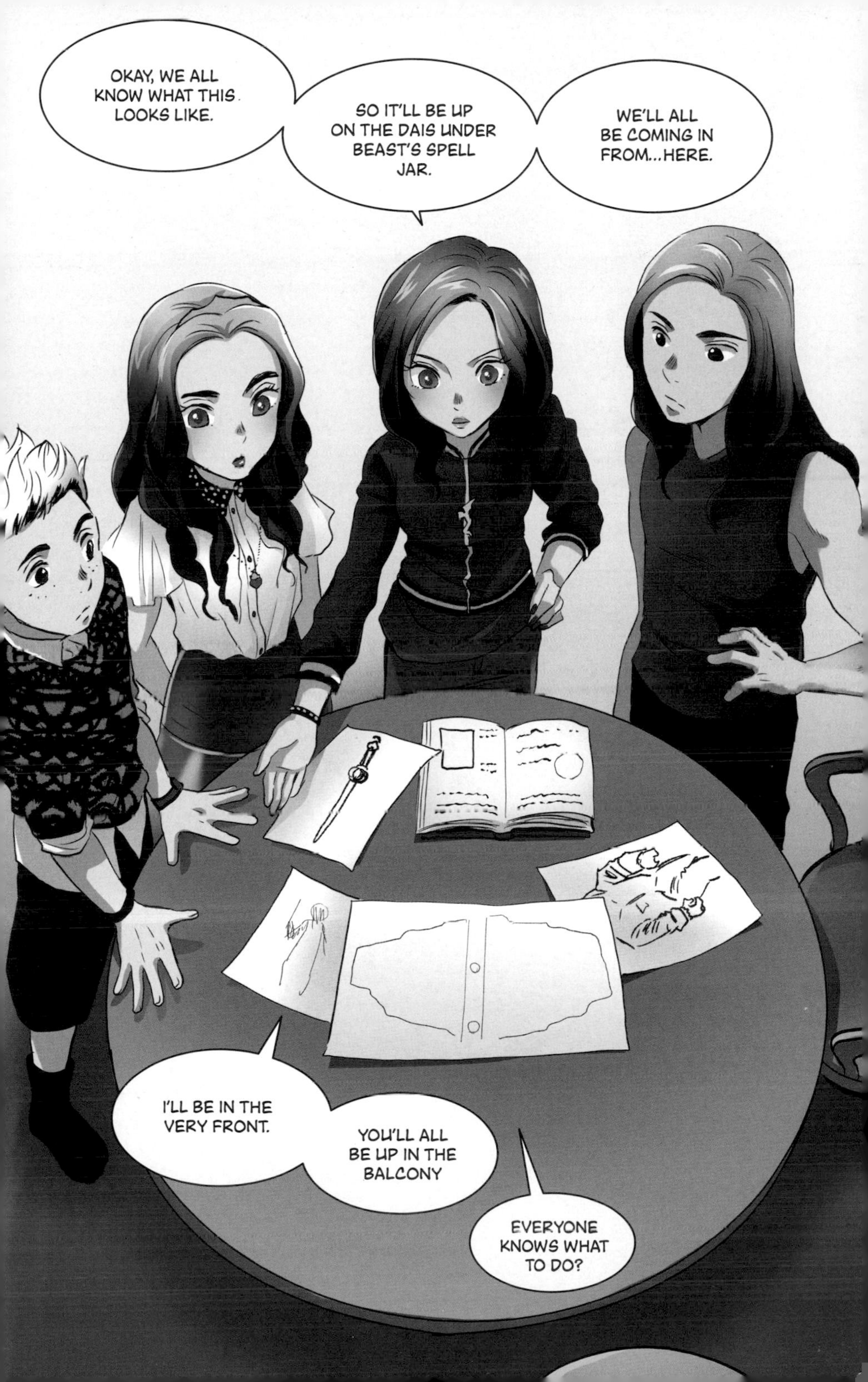
OKAY, WE ALL KNOW WHAT THIS LOOKS LIKE.
SO IT'LL BE UP ON THE DAIS UNDER BEAST'S SPELL JAR.
WE'LL ALL BE COMING IN FROM...HERE.
I'LL BE IN THE VERY FRONT.
YOU'LL ALL BE UP IN THE BALCONY
EVERYONE KNOWS WHAT TO DO?

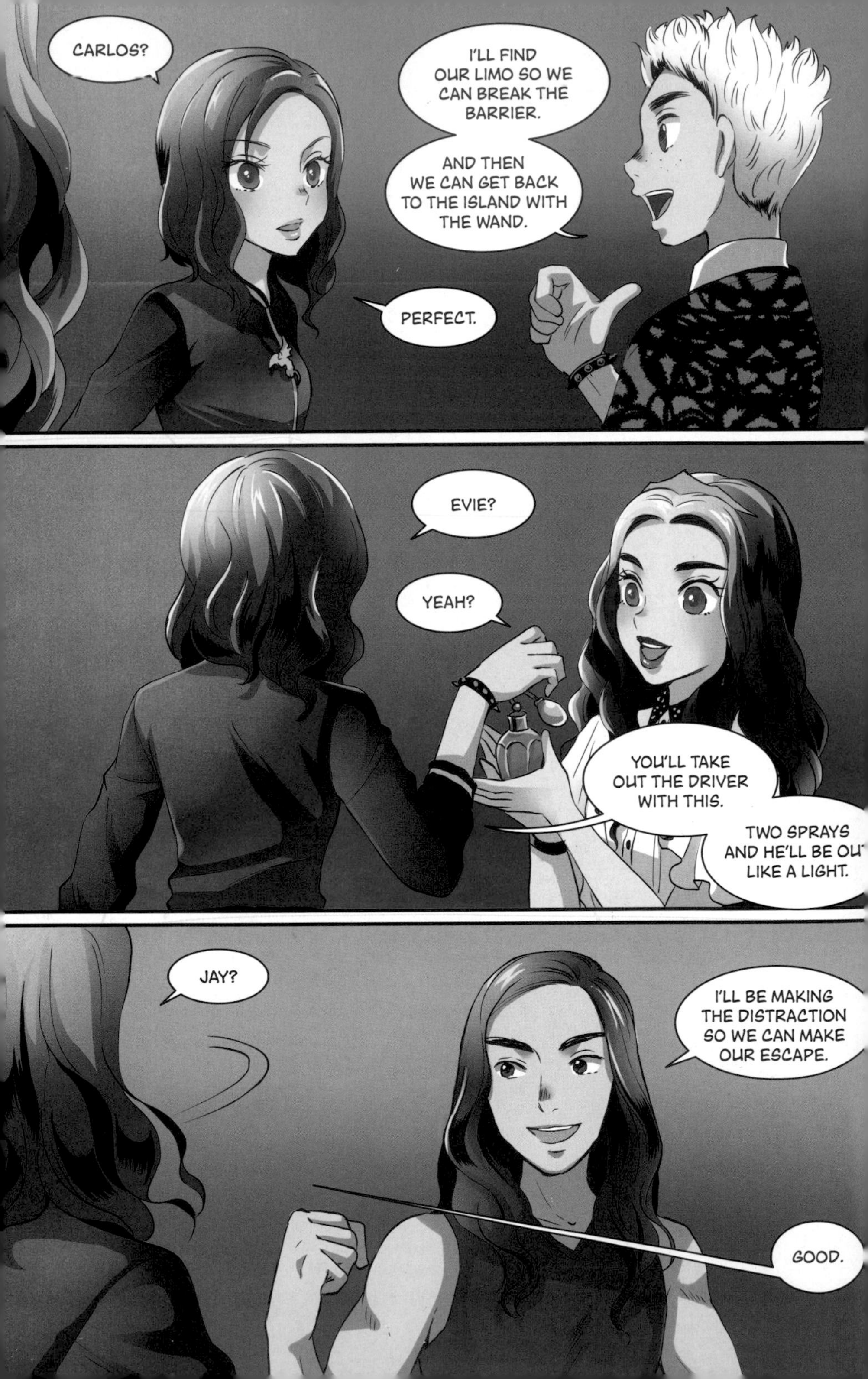
CARLOS?
I'LL FIND OUR LIMO SO WE CAN BREAK THE BARRIER.
AND THEN WE CAN GET BACK TO THE ISLAND WITH THE WAND.
PERFECT.
EVIE?
YEAH?
YOU'LL TAKE OUT THE DRIVER WITH THIS.
TWO SPRAYS AND HE'LL BE OUT LIKE A LIGHT.
JAY?
I'LL BE MAKING THE DISTRACTION SO WE CAN MAKE OUR ESCAPE.
GOOD.

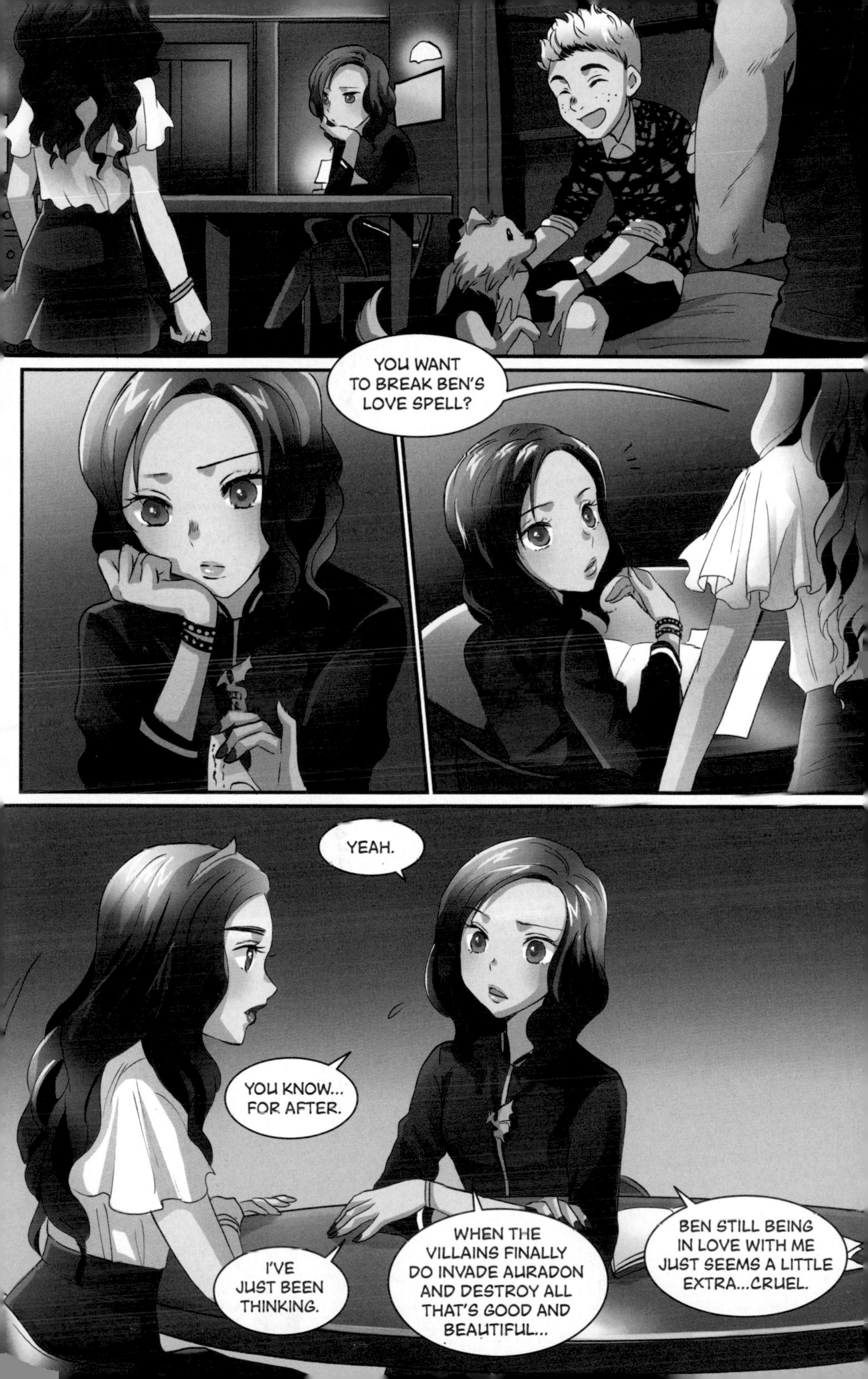
YOU WANT TO BREAK BEN'S LOVE SPELL?
YEAH.
YOU KNOW... FOR AFTER.
I'VE JUST BEEN THINKING.
WHEN THE VILLAINS FINALLY DO INVADE AURADON AND DESTROY ALL THAT'S GOOD AND BEAUTIFUL...
BEN STILL BEING IN LOVE WITH ME JUST SEEMS A LITTLE EXTRA...CRUEL.

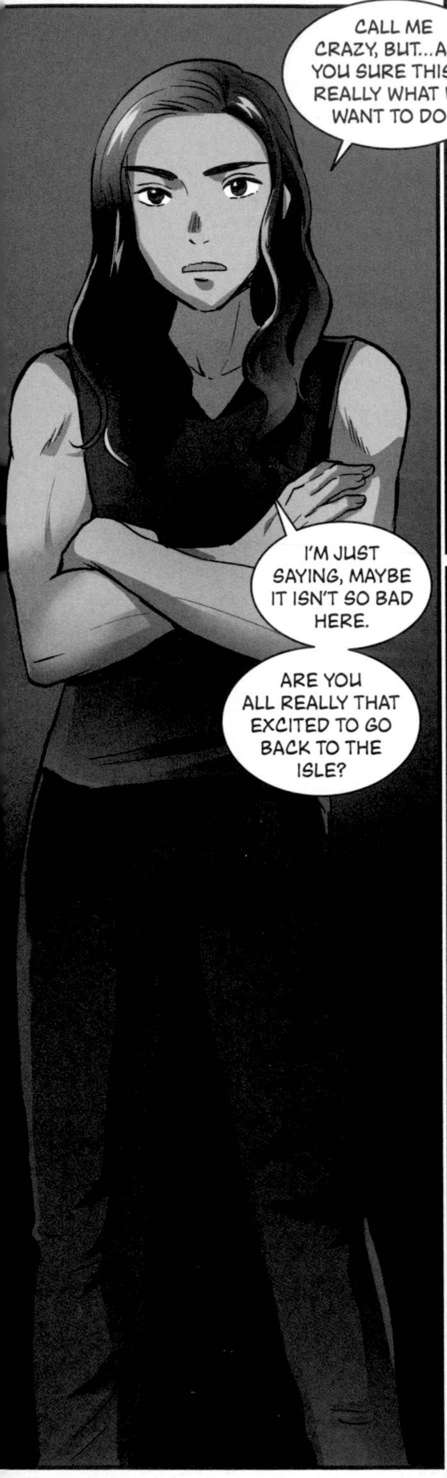
CALL ME CRAZY, BUT...ARE YOU SURE THIS IS REALLY WHAT WE WANT TO DO?
I'M JUST SAYING, MAYBE IT ISN'T SO BAD HERE.
ARE YOU ALL REALLY THAT EXCITED TO GO BACK TO THE ISLE?
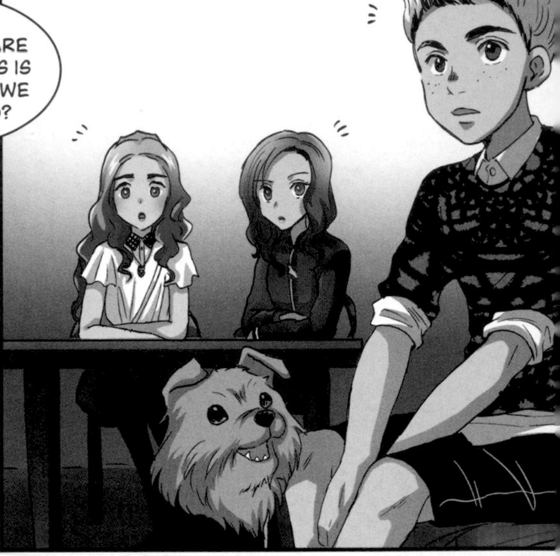
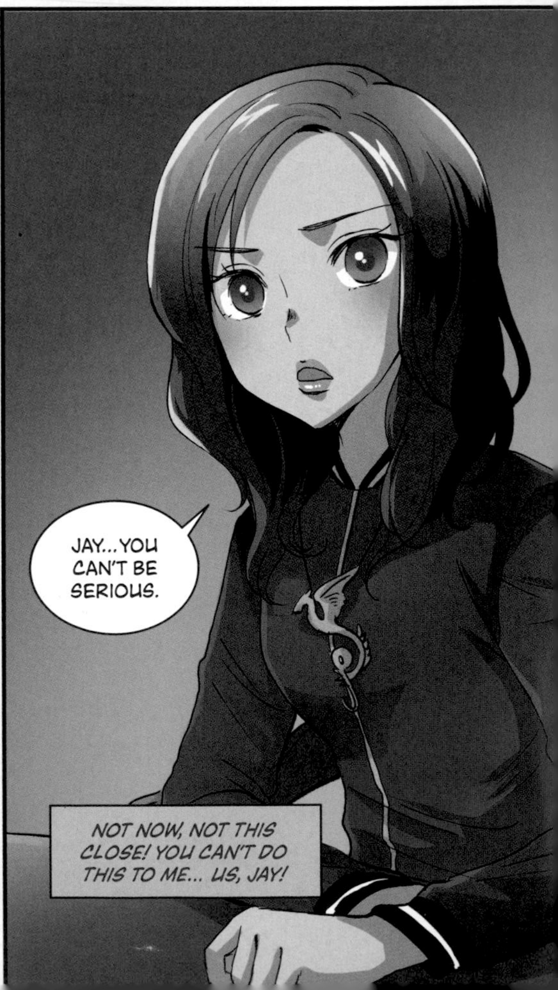
JAY...YOU CAN'T BE SERIOUS.
NOT NOW, NOT THIS CLOSE! YOU CAN'T DO THIS TO ME... US, JAY!

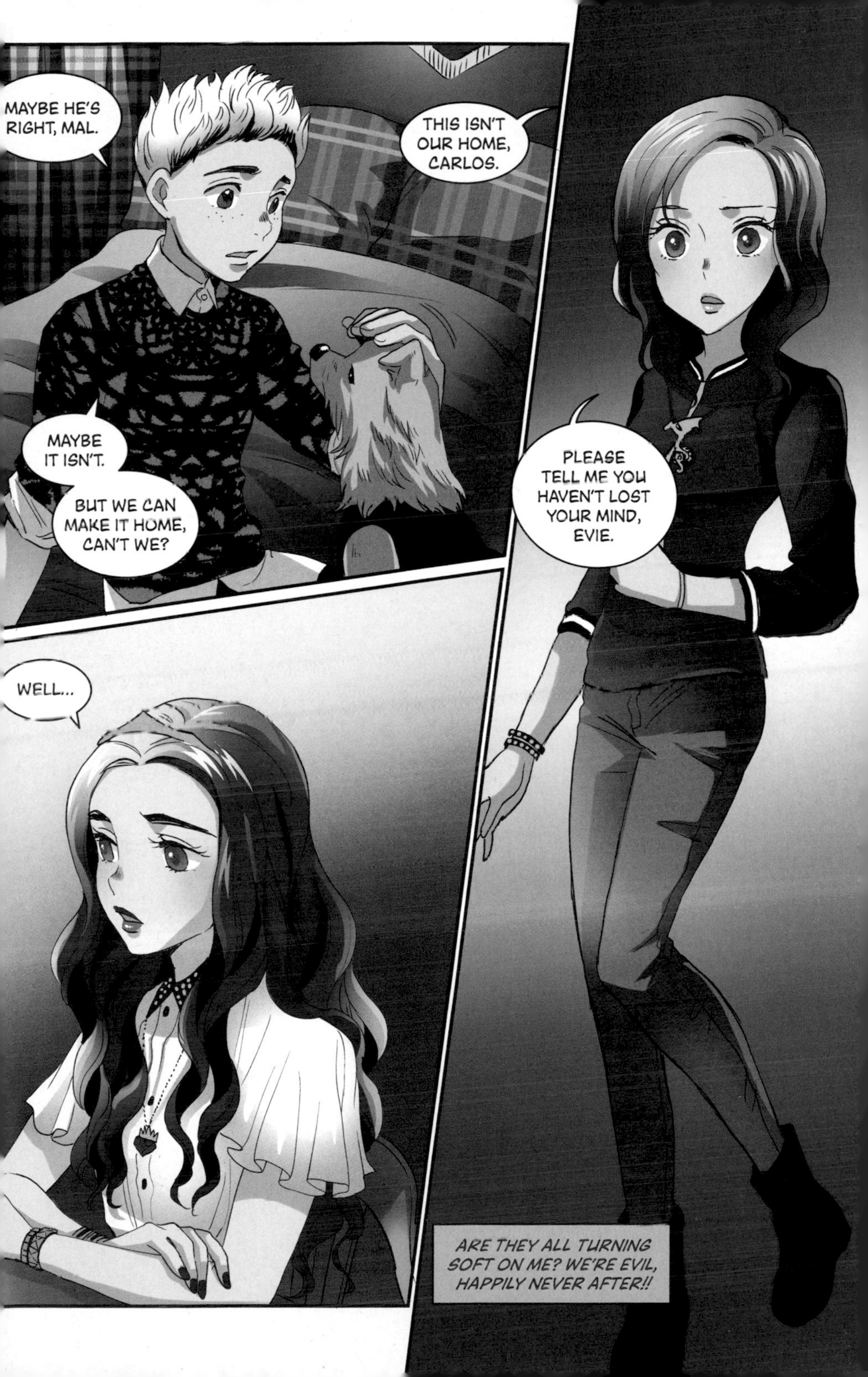
MAYBE HE'S RIGHT, MAL.
THIS ISN'T OUR HOME, CARLOS.
MAYBE IT ISN'T.
BUT WE CAN MAKE IT HOME, CAN'T WE?
WELL...
PLEASE TELL ME YOU HAVEN'T LOST YOUR MIND, EVIE.
ARE THEY ALL TURNING SOFT ON ME? WE'RE EVIL, HAPPILY NEVER AFTER!!

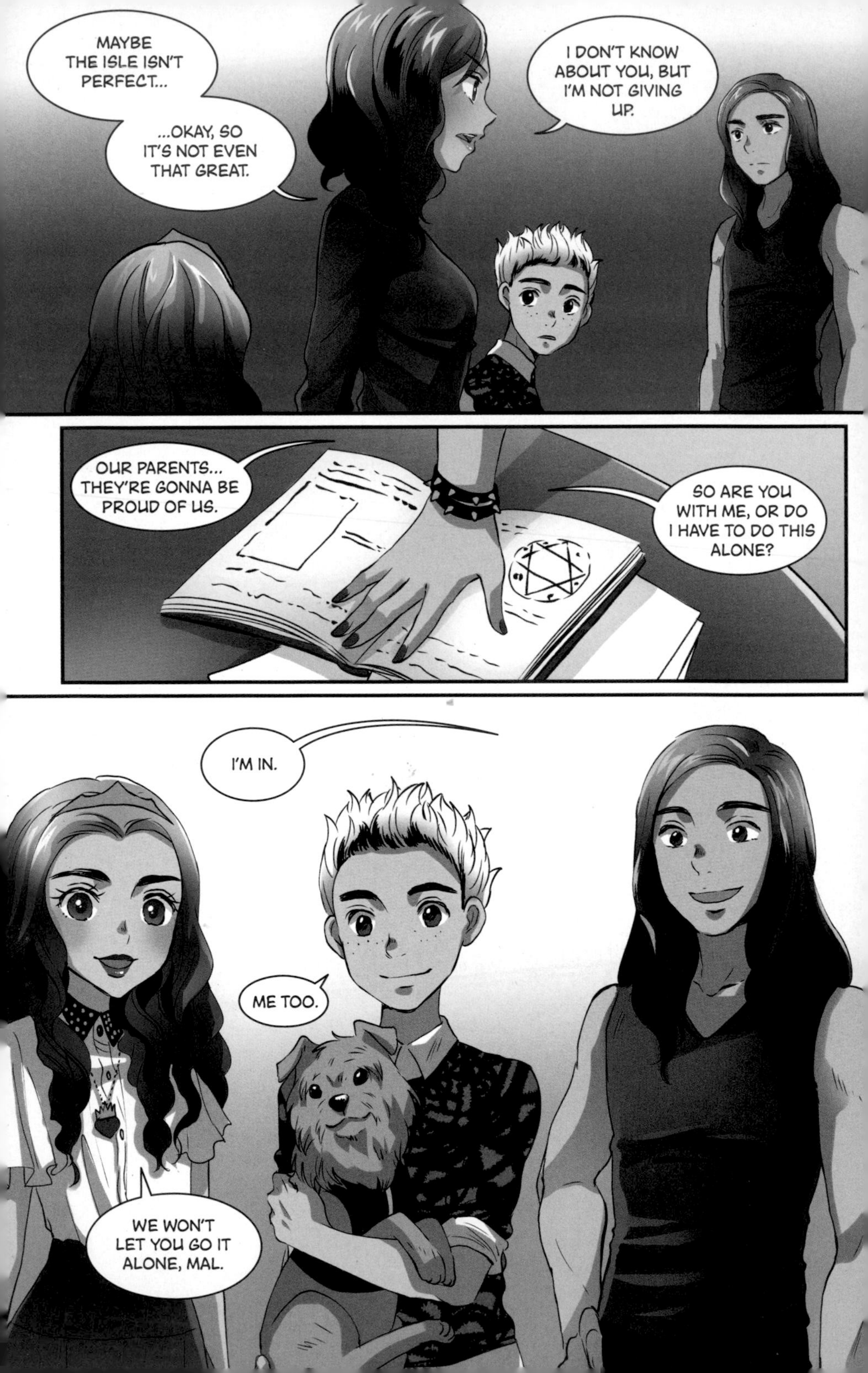
MAYBE THE ISLE ISN'T PERFECT...
...OKAY, SO IT'S NOT EVEN THAT GREAT.
I DON'T KNOW ABOUT YOU, BUT I'M NOT GIVING UP.
OUR PARENTS... THEY'RE GONNA BE PROUD OF US.
SO ARE YOU WITH ME, OR DO I HAVE TO DO THIS ALONE?
I'M IN.
ME TOO.
WE WON'T LET YOU GO IT ALONE, MAL.

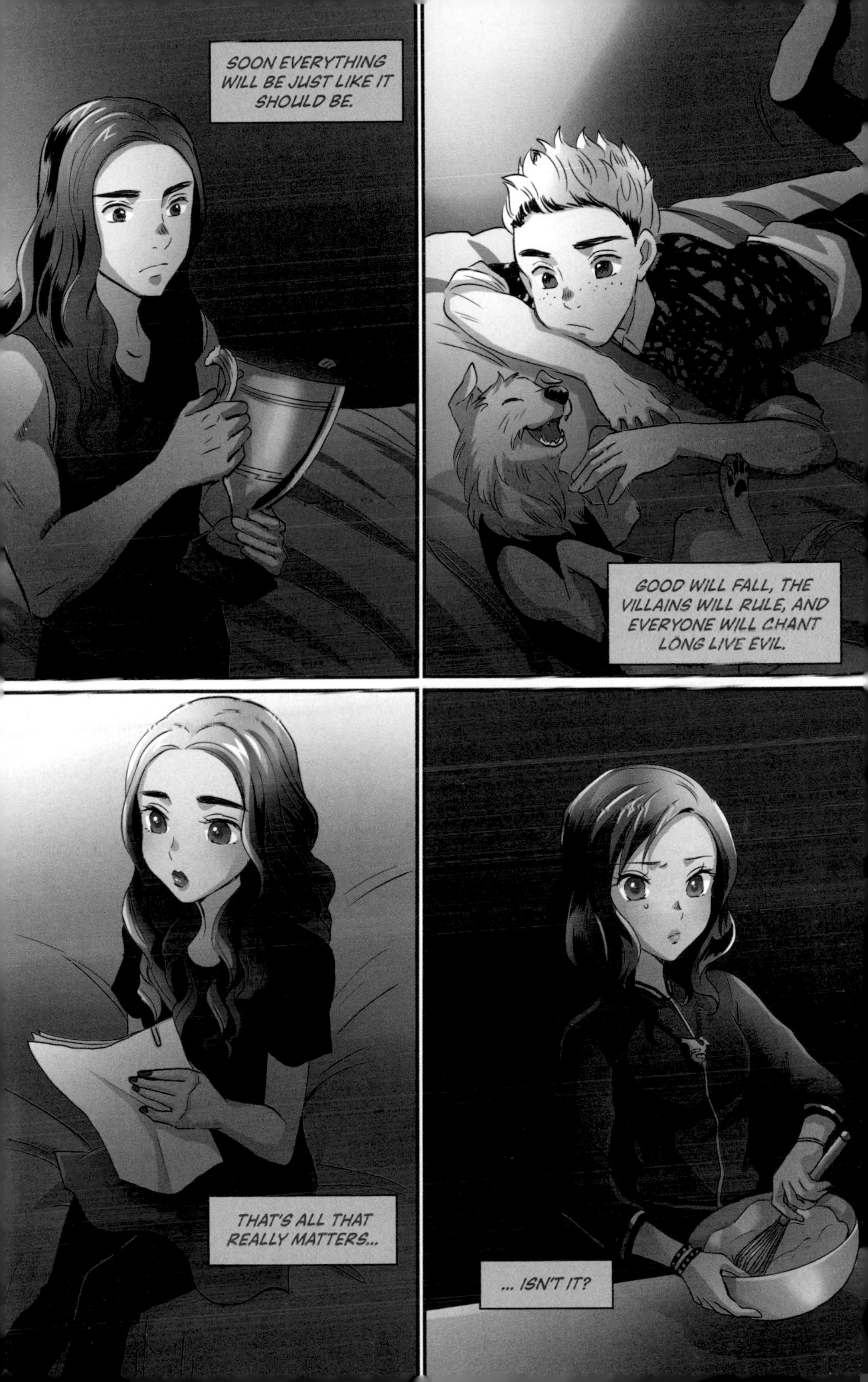
SOON EVERYTHING WILL BE JUST LIKE IT SHOULD BE.
GOOD WILL FALL, THE VILLAINS WILL RULE, AND EVERYONE WILL CHANT LONG LIVE EVIL.
THAT'S ALL THAT REALLY MATTERS...
... ISN'T IT?

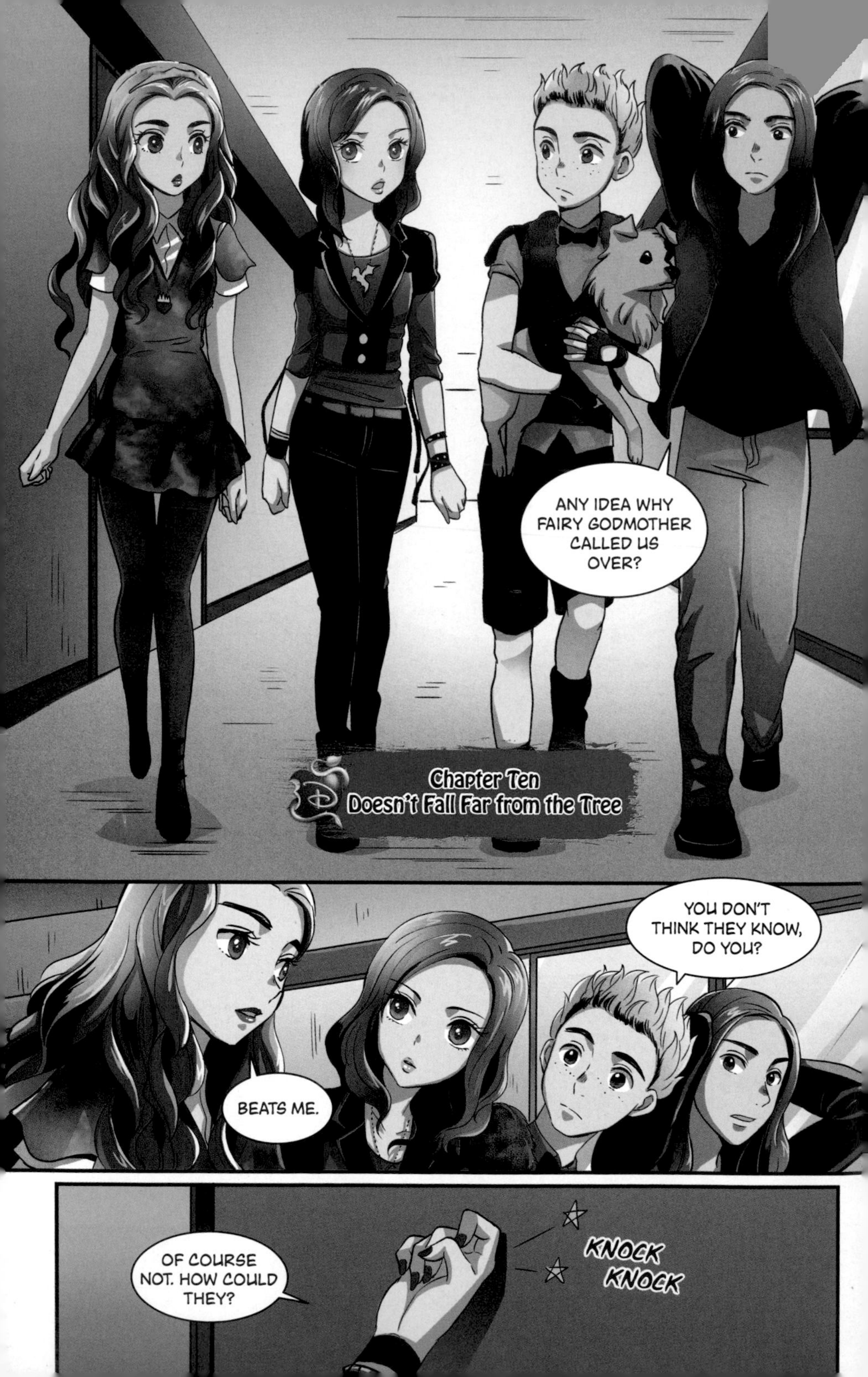
ANY IDEA WHY FAIRY GODMOTHER CALLED US OVER?
Chapter Ten
Doesn't Fall Far from the Tree
BEATS ME.
YOU DON'T THINK THEY KNOW, DO YOU?
OF COURSE NOT. HOW COULD THEY?
KNOCK KNOCK

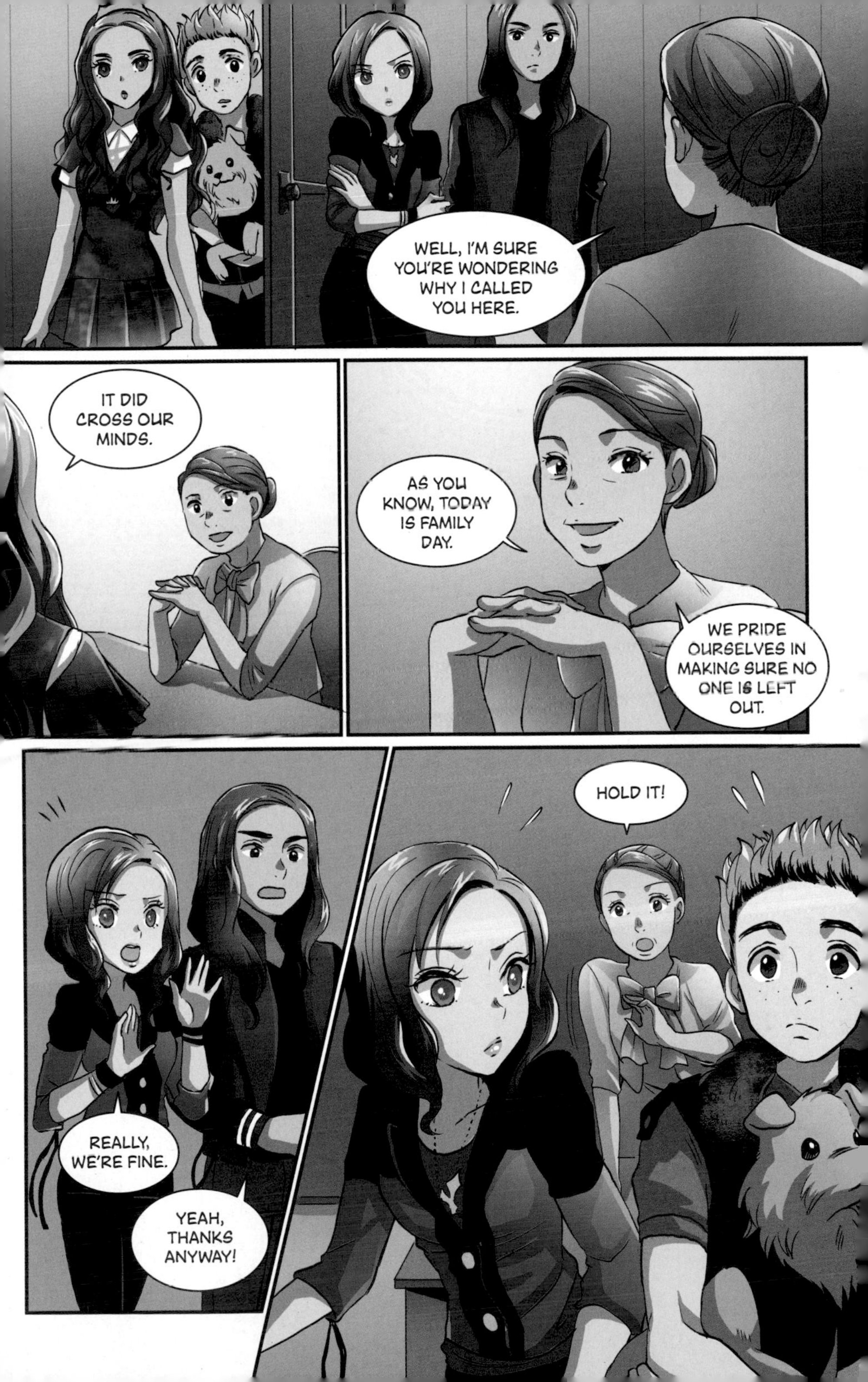
WELL, I'M SURE YOU'RE WONDERING WHY I CALLED YOU HERE.
IT DID CROSS OUR MINDS.
AS YOU KNOW, TODAY IS FAMILY DAY.
WE PRIDE OURSELVES IN MAKING SURE NO ONE IS LEFT OUT.
REALLY, WE'RE FINE.
YEAH, THANKS ANYWAY!
HOLD IT!

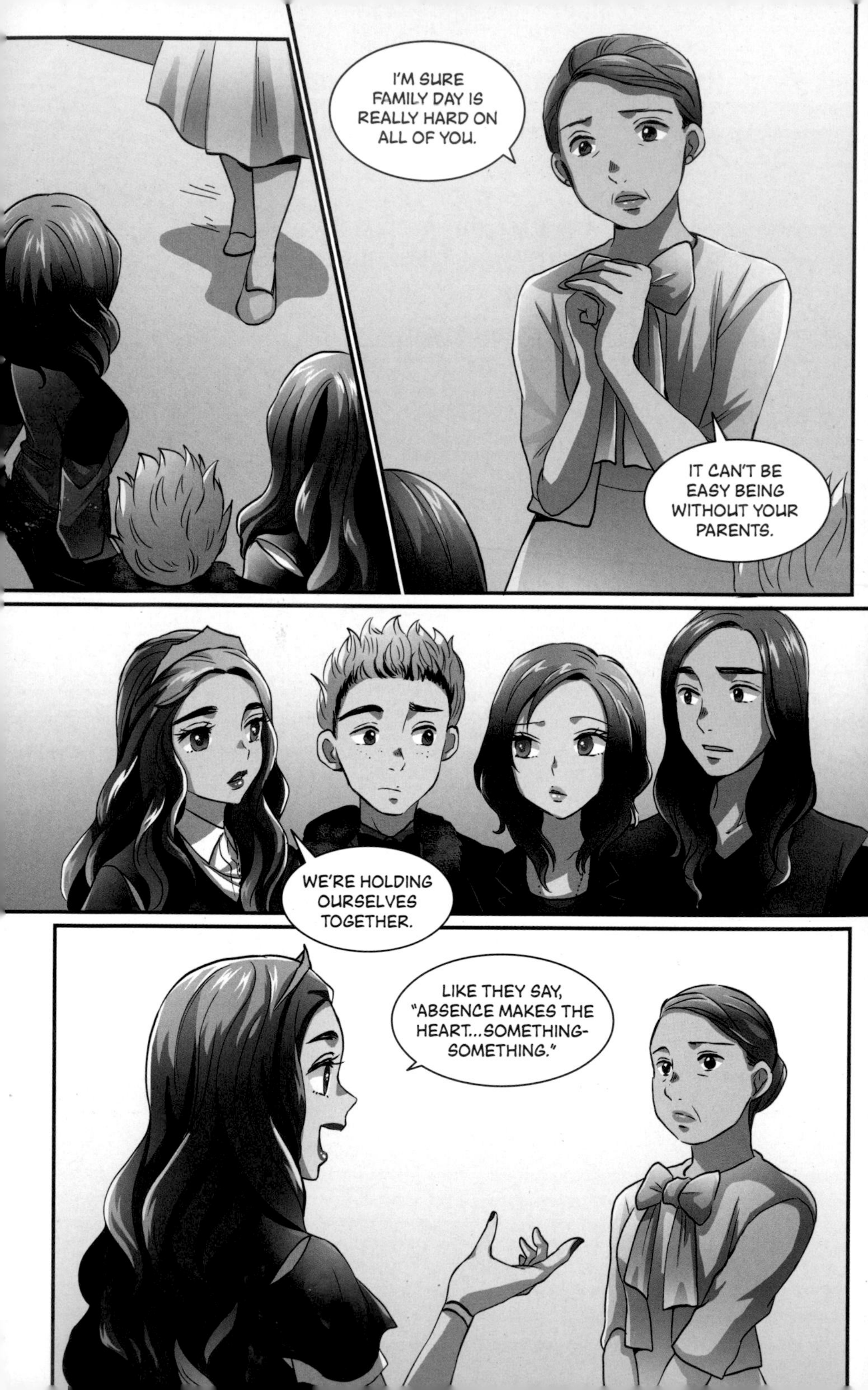
I'M SURE FAMILY DAY IS REALLY HARD ON ALL OF YOU.
IT CAN'T BE EASY BEING WITHOUT YOUR PARENTS.
WE'RE HOLDING OURSELVES TOGETHER.
LIKE THEY SAY, "ABSENCE MAKES THE HEART...SOMETHING-SOMETHING."

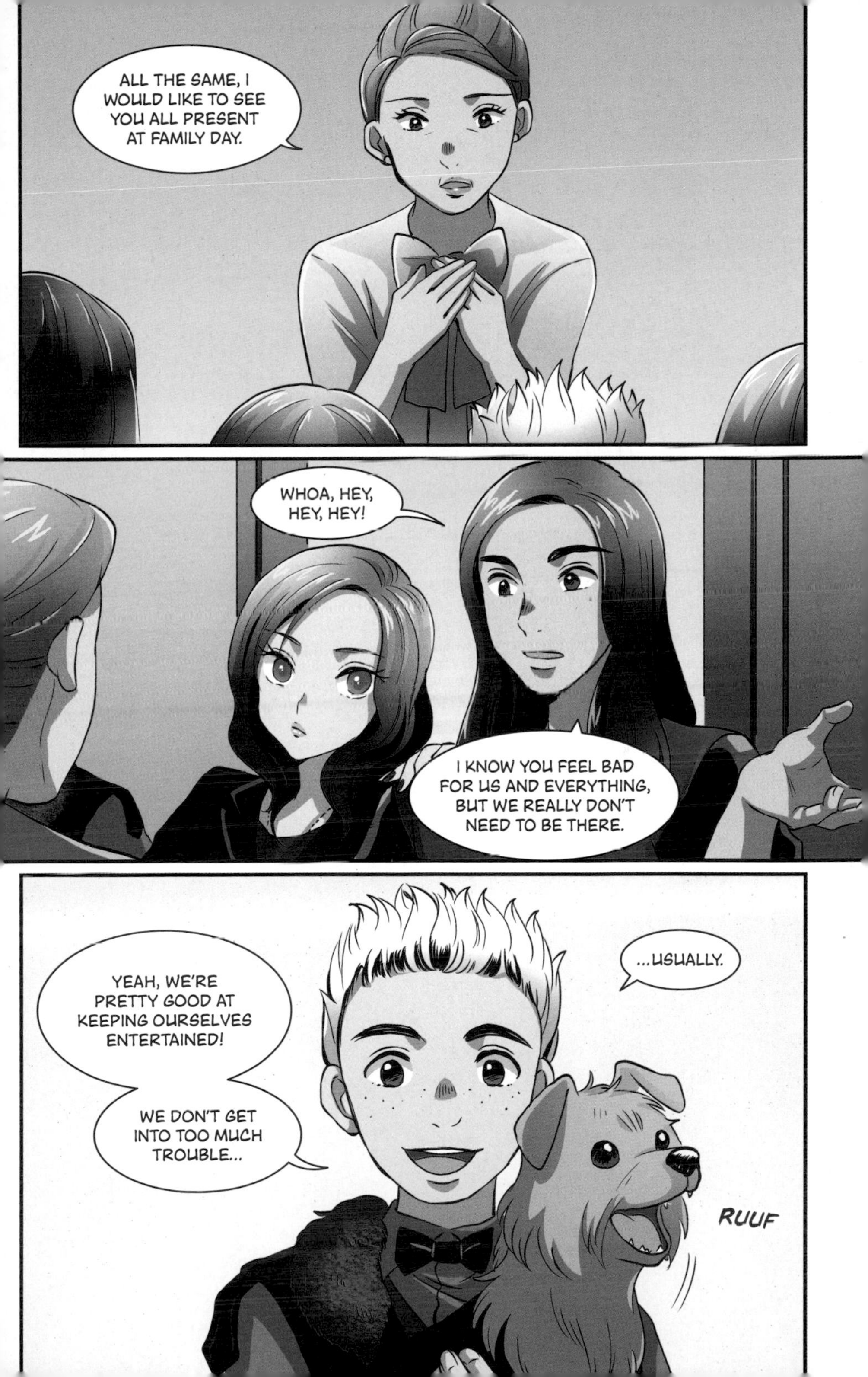
ALL THE SAME, I WOULD LIKE TO SEE YOU ALL PRESENT AT FAMILY DAY.
WHOA, HEY, HEY, HEY!
I KNOW YOU FEEL BAD FOR US AND EVERYTHING, BUT WE REALLY DON'T NEED TO BE THERE.
YEAH, WE'RE PRETTY GOOD AT KEEPING OURSELVES ENTERTAINED!
WE DON'T GET INTO TOO MUCH TROUBLE...
...USUALLY.
RUUF

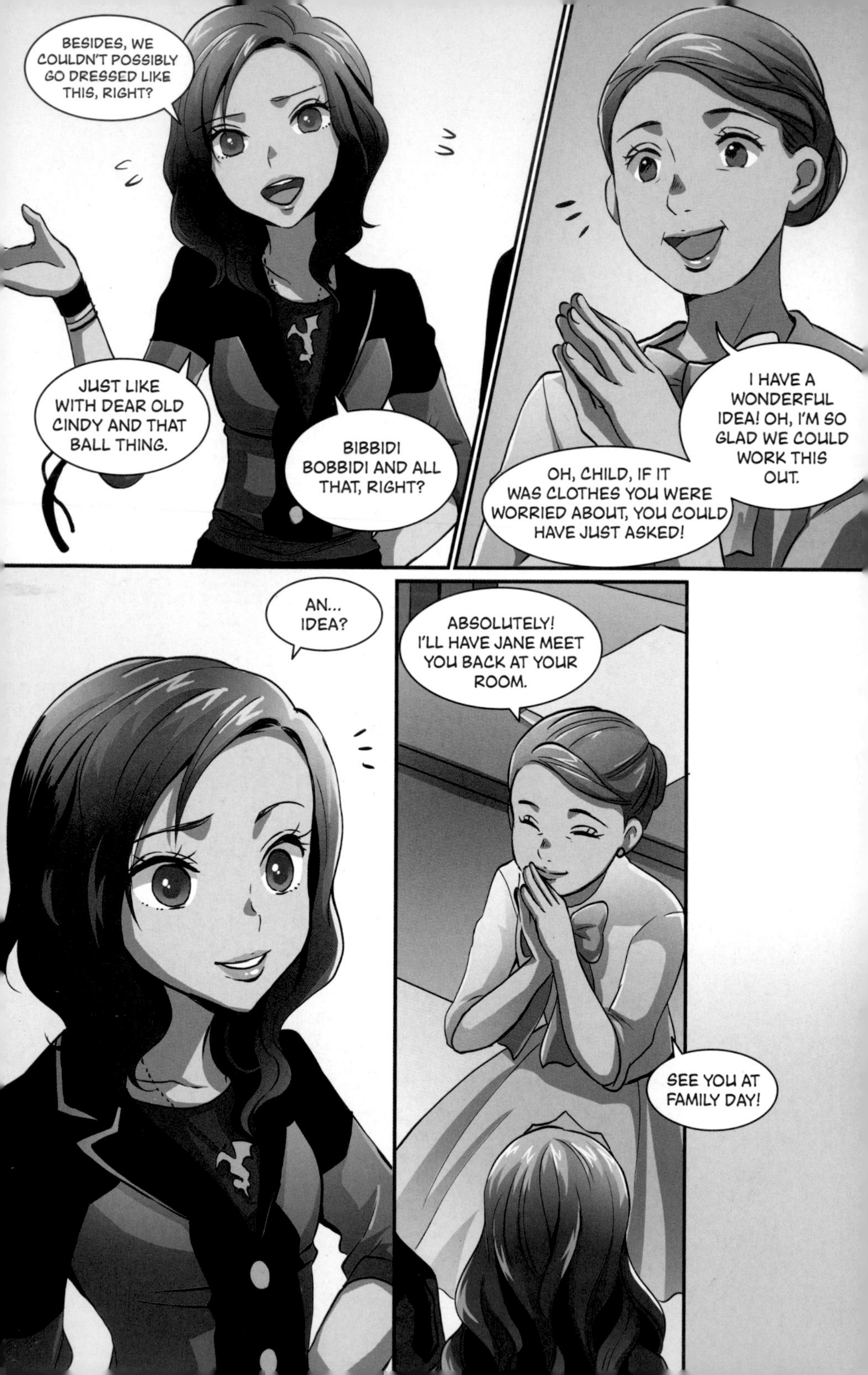
BESIDES, WE COULDN'T POSSIBLY GO DRESSED LIKE THIS, RIGHT?
JUST LIKE WITH DEAR OLD CINDY AND THAT BALL THING.
BIBBIDI BOBBIDI AND ALL THAT, RIGHT?
OH, CHILD, IF IT WAS CLOTHES YOU WERE WORRIED ABOUT, YOU COULD HAVE JUST ASKED!
I HAVE A WONDERFUL IDEA! OH, I'M SO GLAD WE COULD WORK THIS OUT.
AN... IDEA?
ABSOLUTELY! I'LL HAVE JANE MEET YOU BACK AT YOUR ROOM.
SEE YOU AT FAMILY DAY!

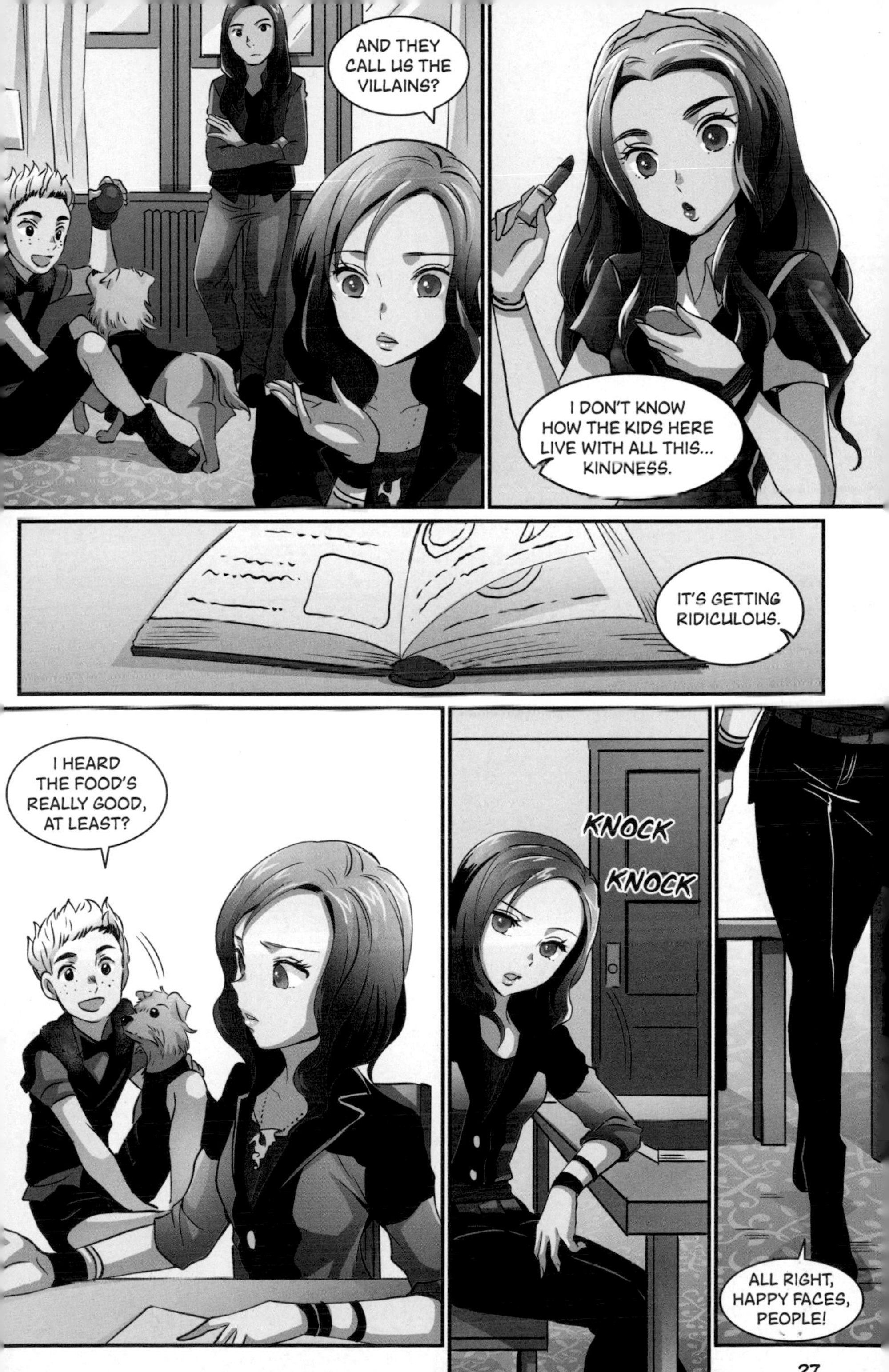
AND THEY CALL US THE VILLAINS?
I DON'T KNOW HOW THE KIDS HERE LIVE WITH ALL THIS... KINDNESS.
IT'S GETTING RIDICULOUS.
I HEARD THE FOOD'S REALLY GOOD, AT LEAST?
KNOCK
KNOCK
ALL RIGHT, HAPPY FACES, PEOPLE!

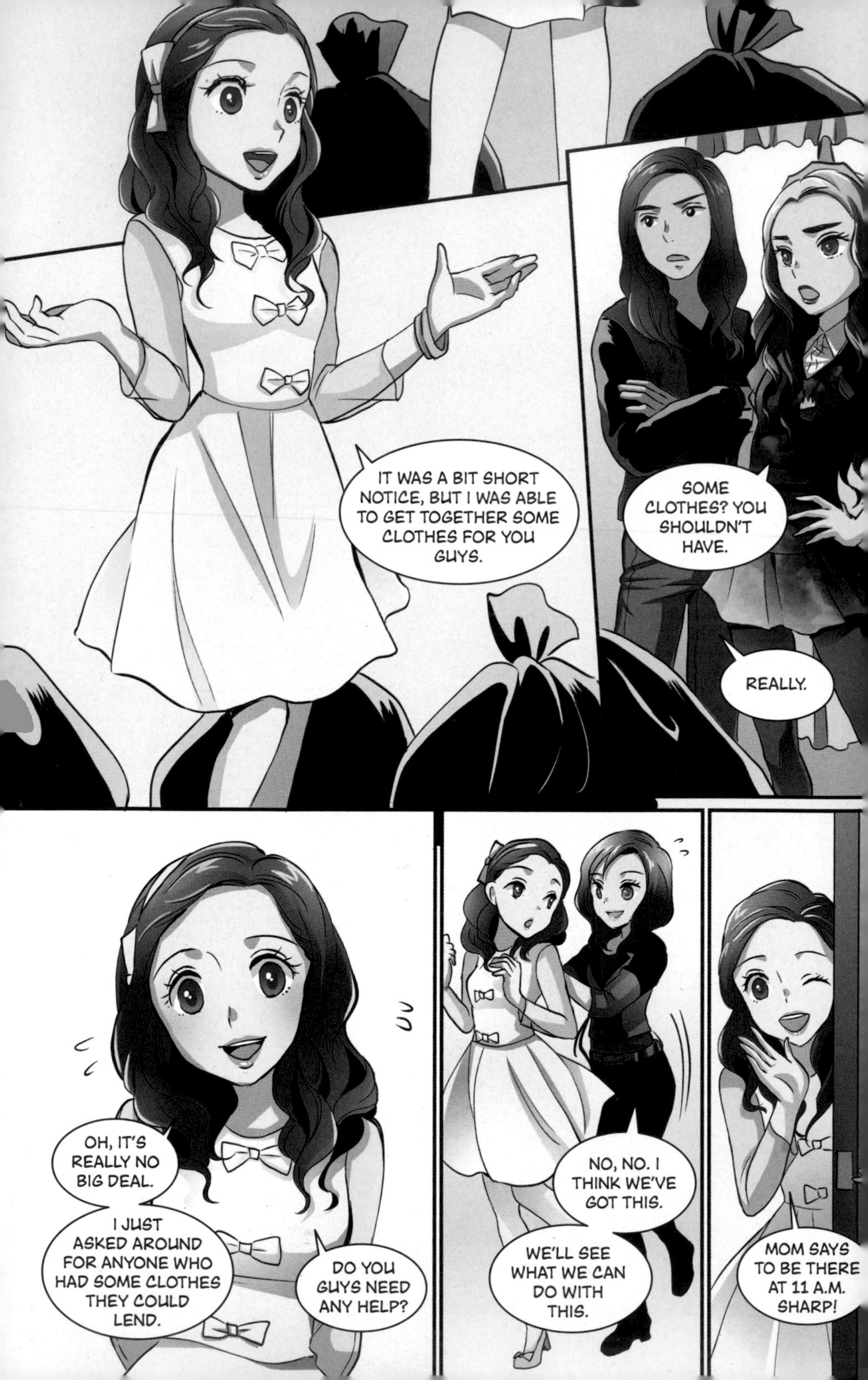
IT WAS A BIT SHORT NOTICE, BUT I WAS ABLE TO GET TOGETHER SOME CLOTHES FOR YOU GUYS.
SOME CLOTHES? YOU SHOULDN'T HAVE.
REALLY.
OH, IT'S REALLY NO BIG DEAL.
I JUST ASKED AROUND FOR ANYONE WHO HAD SOME CLOTHES THEY COULD LEND.
DO YOU GUYS NEED ANY HELP?
NO, NO. I THINK WE'VE GOT THIS.
WE'LL SEE WHAT WE CAN DO WITH THIS.
MOM SAYS TO BE THERE AT 11 A.M. SHARP!

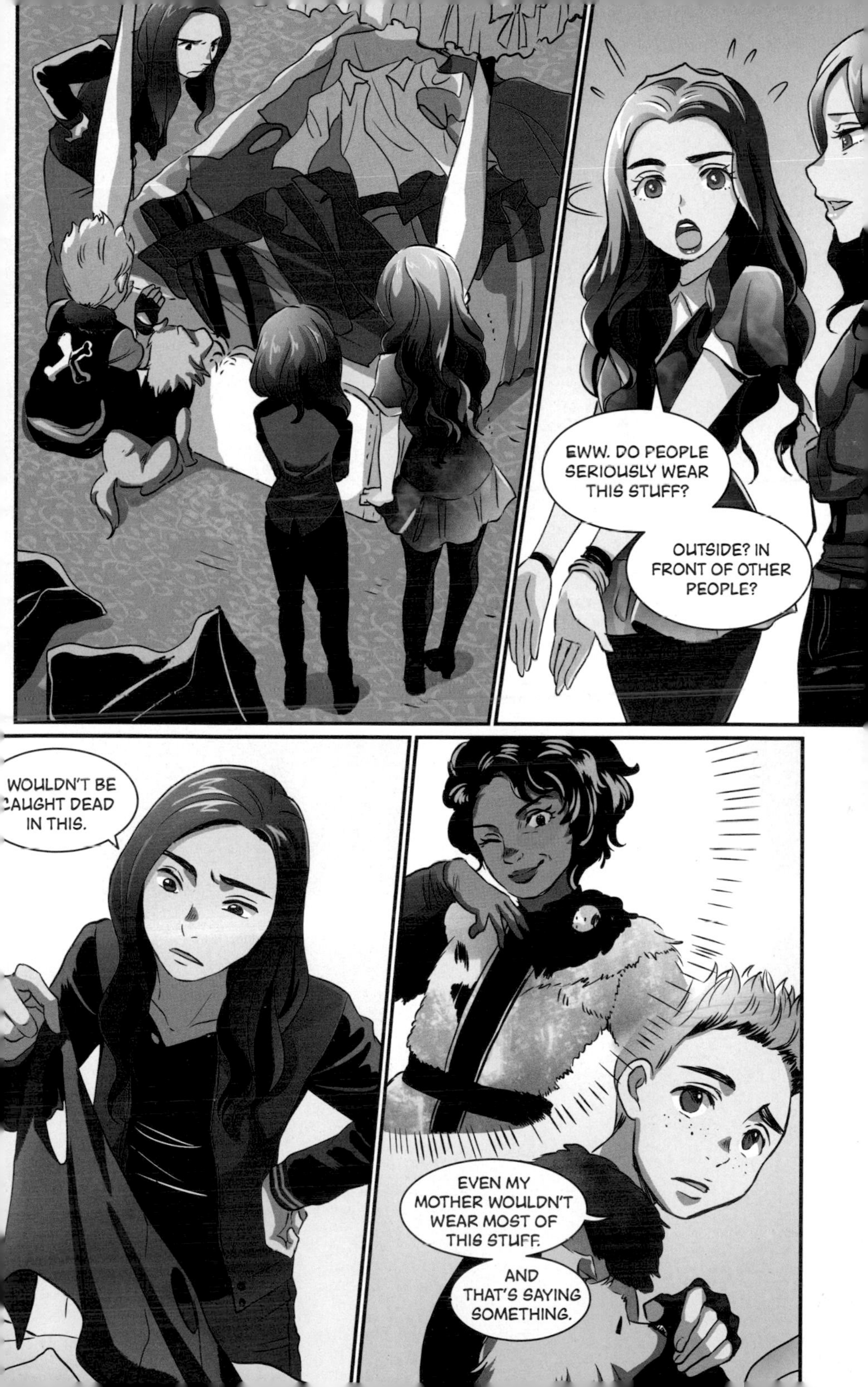
EWW. DO PEOPLE SERIOUSLY WEAR THIS STUFF?
OUTSIDE? IN FRONT OF OTHER PEOPLE?
WOULDN'T BE CAUGHT DEAD IN THIS.
EVEN MY MOTHER WOULDN'T WEAR MOST OF THIS STUFF.
AND THAT'S SAYING SOMETHING.

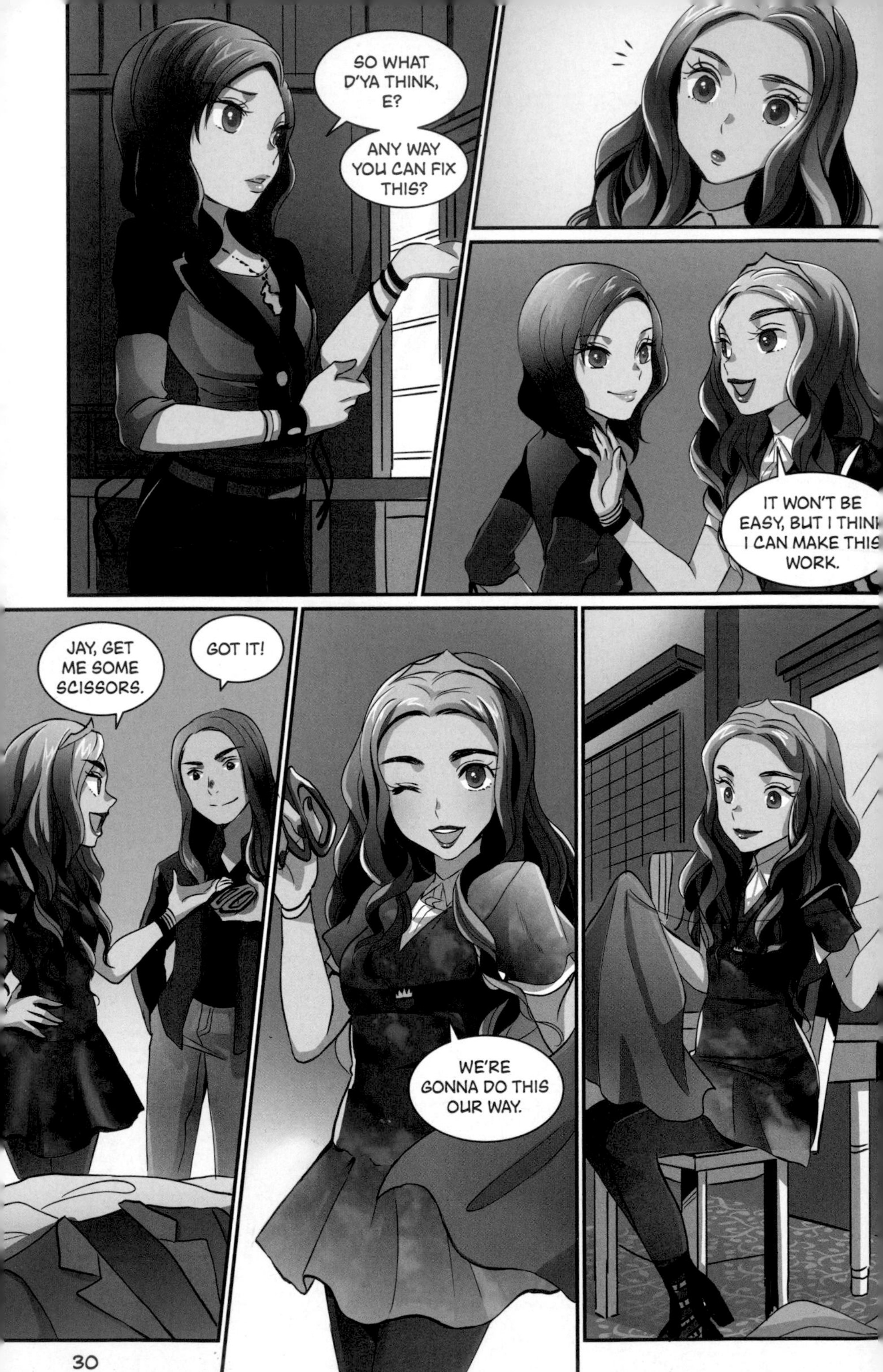
SO WHAT D'YA THINK, E?
ANY WAY YOU CAN FIX THIS?
IT WON'T BE EASY, BUT I THINK I CAN MAKE THIS WORK.
JAY, GET ME SOME SCISSORS.
GOT IT!
WE'RE GONNA DO THIS OUR WAY.

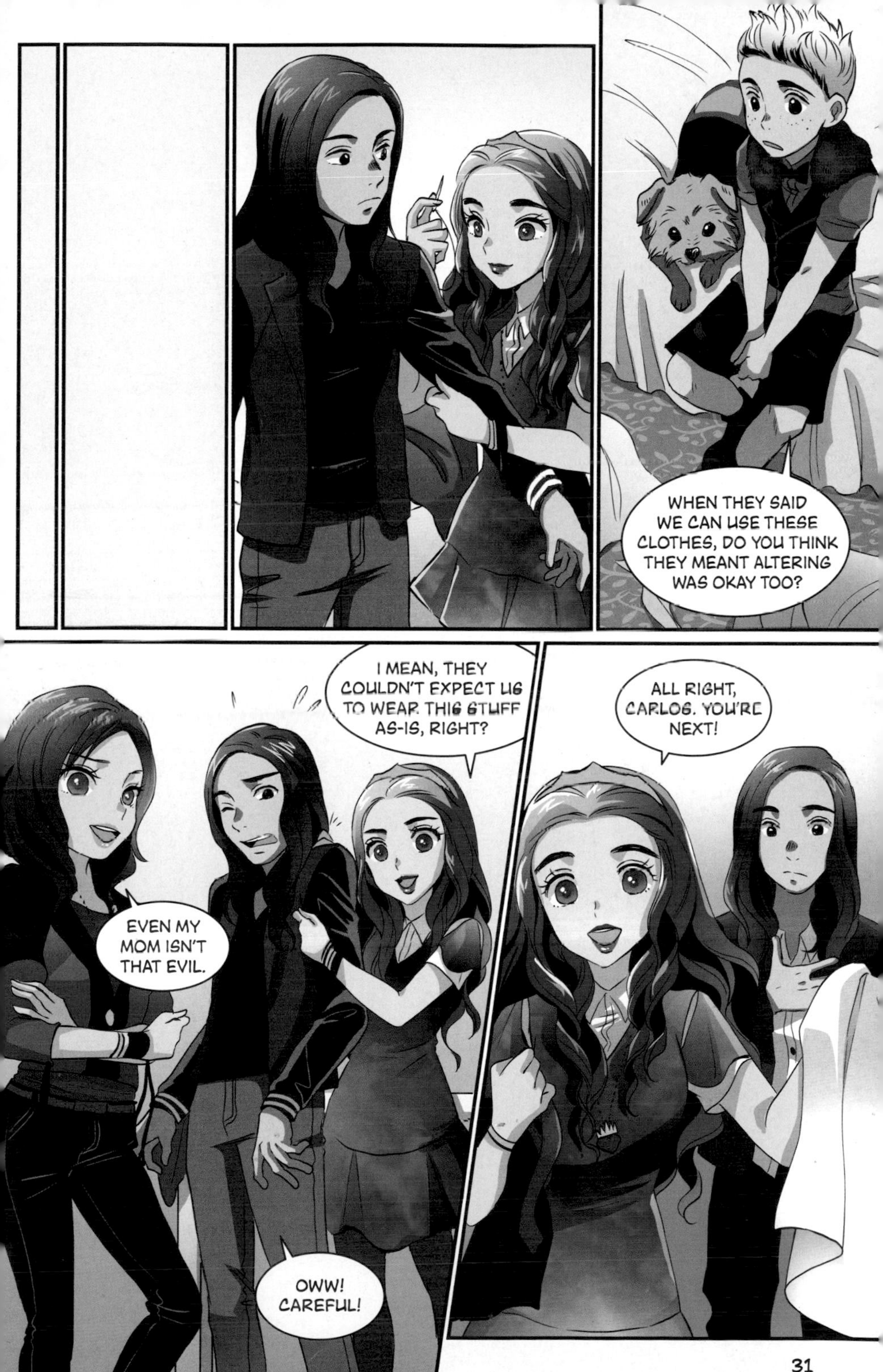
WHEN THEY SAID WE CAN USE THESE CLOTHES, DO YOU THINK THEY MEANT ALTERING WAS OKAY TOO?
I MEAN, THEY COULDN'T EXPECT US TO WEAR THIS STUFF AS-IS, RIGHT?
EVEN MY MOM ISN'T THAT EVIL.
OWW! CAREFUL!
ALL RIGHT, CARLOS. YOU'RE NEXT!

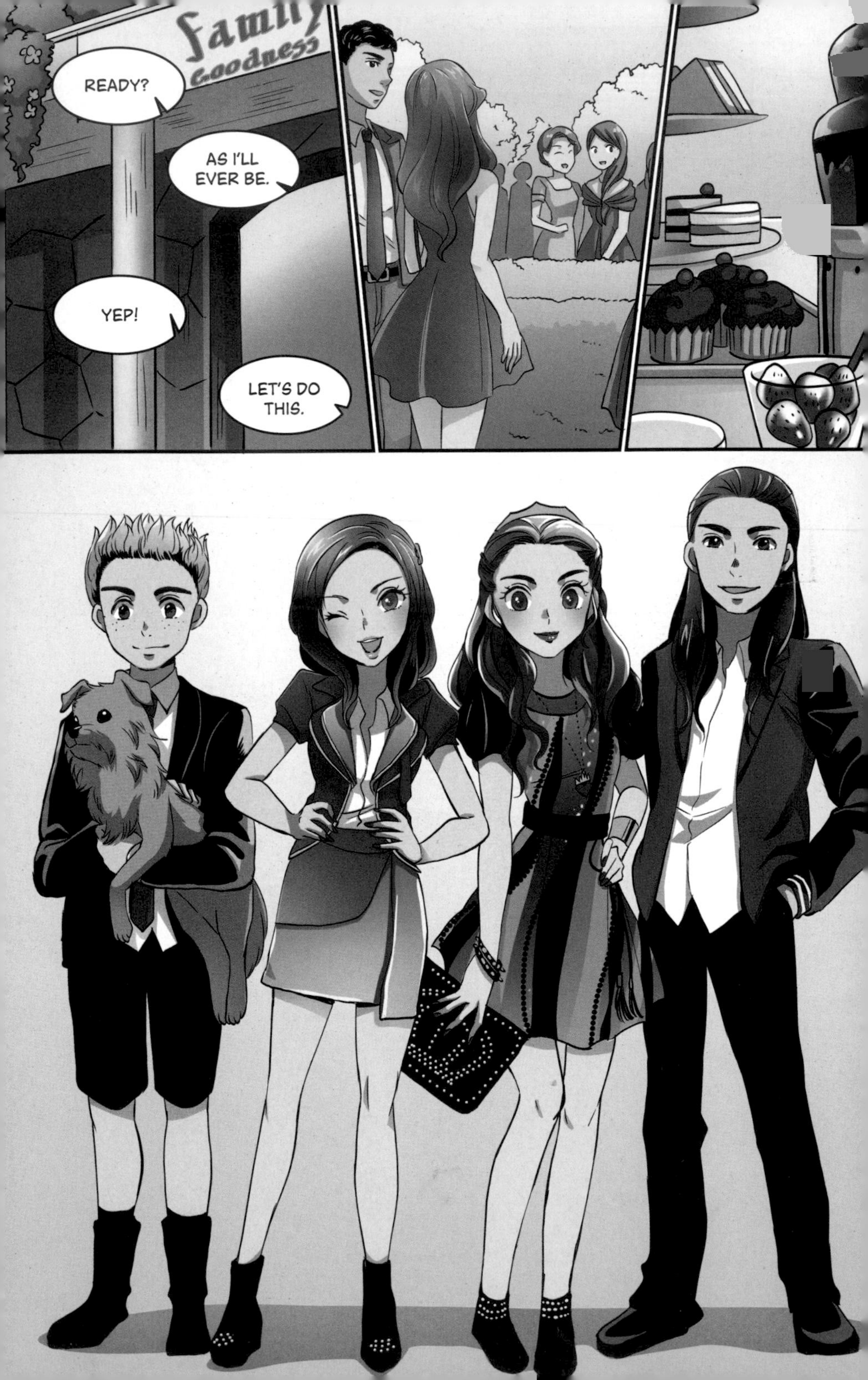
Goodness
READY?
AS I'LL EVER BE.
YEP!
LET'S DO THIS.

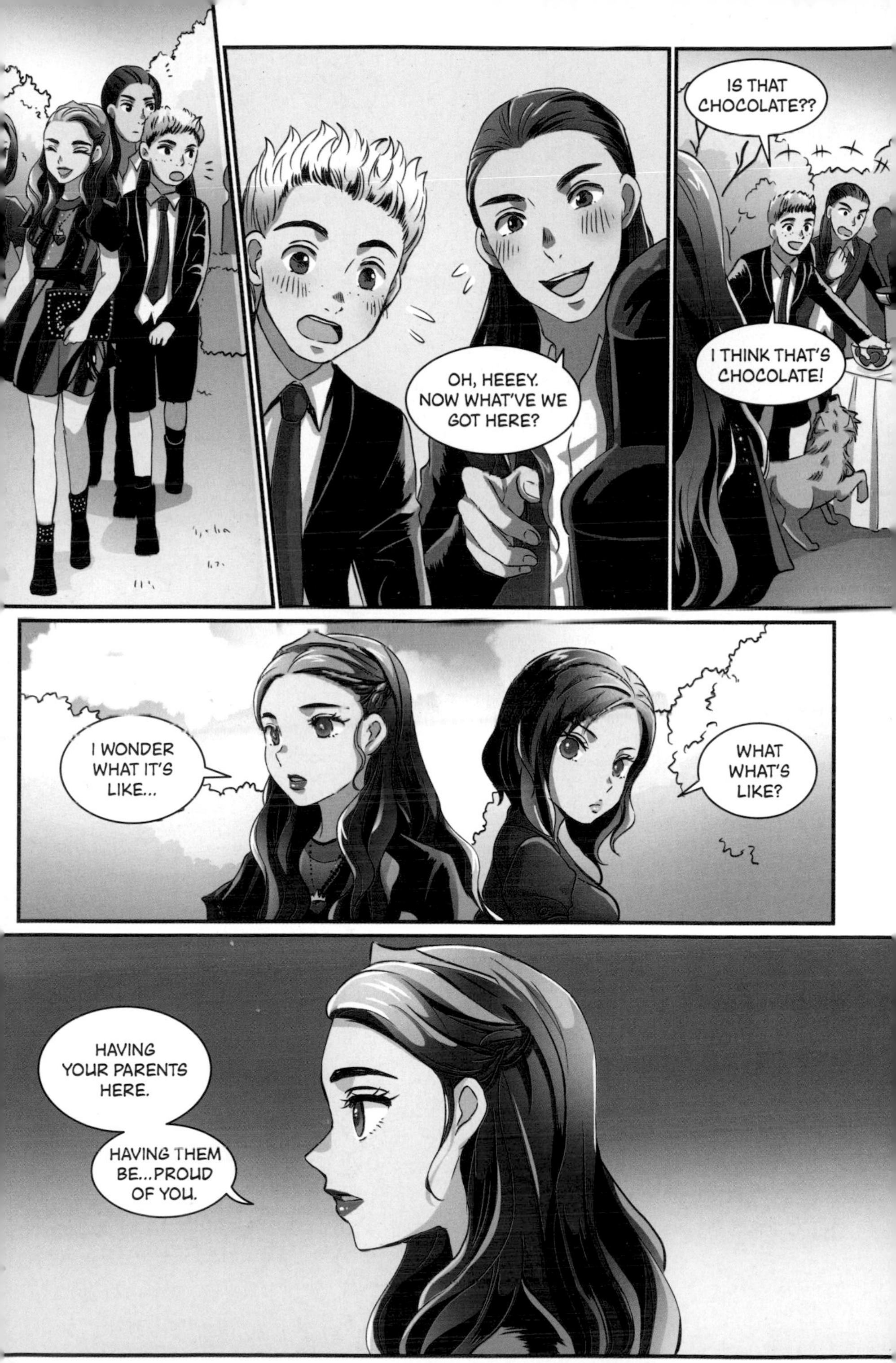
OH, HEEEY. NOW WHAT'VE WE GOT HERE?
IS THAT CHOCOLATE??
I THINK THAT'S CHOCOLATE!
I WONDER WHAT IT'S LIKE...
WHAT WHAT'S LIKE?
HAVING YOUR PARENTS HERE.
HAVING THEM BE...PROUD OF YOU.

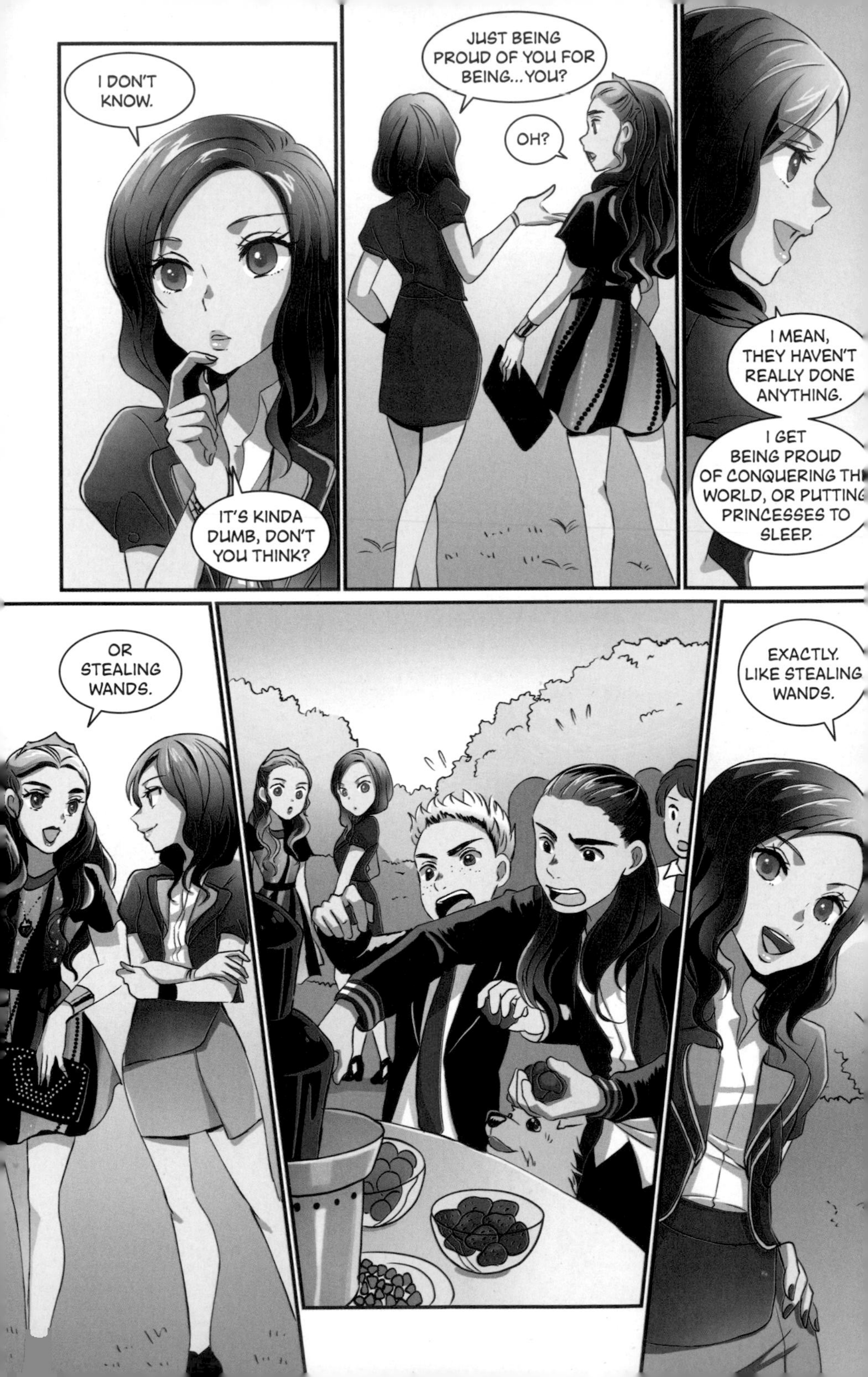
I DON'T KNOW.
IT'S KINDA DUMB, DON'T YOU THINK?
JUST BEING PROUD OF YOU FOR BEING...YOU?
OH?
I MEAN, THEY HAVEN'T REALLY DONE ANYTHING.
I GET BEING PROUD OF CONQUERING THE WORLD, OR PUTTING PRINCESSES TO SLEEP.
OR STEALING WANDS.
EXACTLY. LIKE STEALING WANDS.

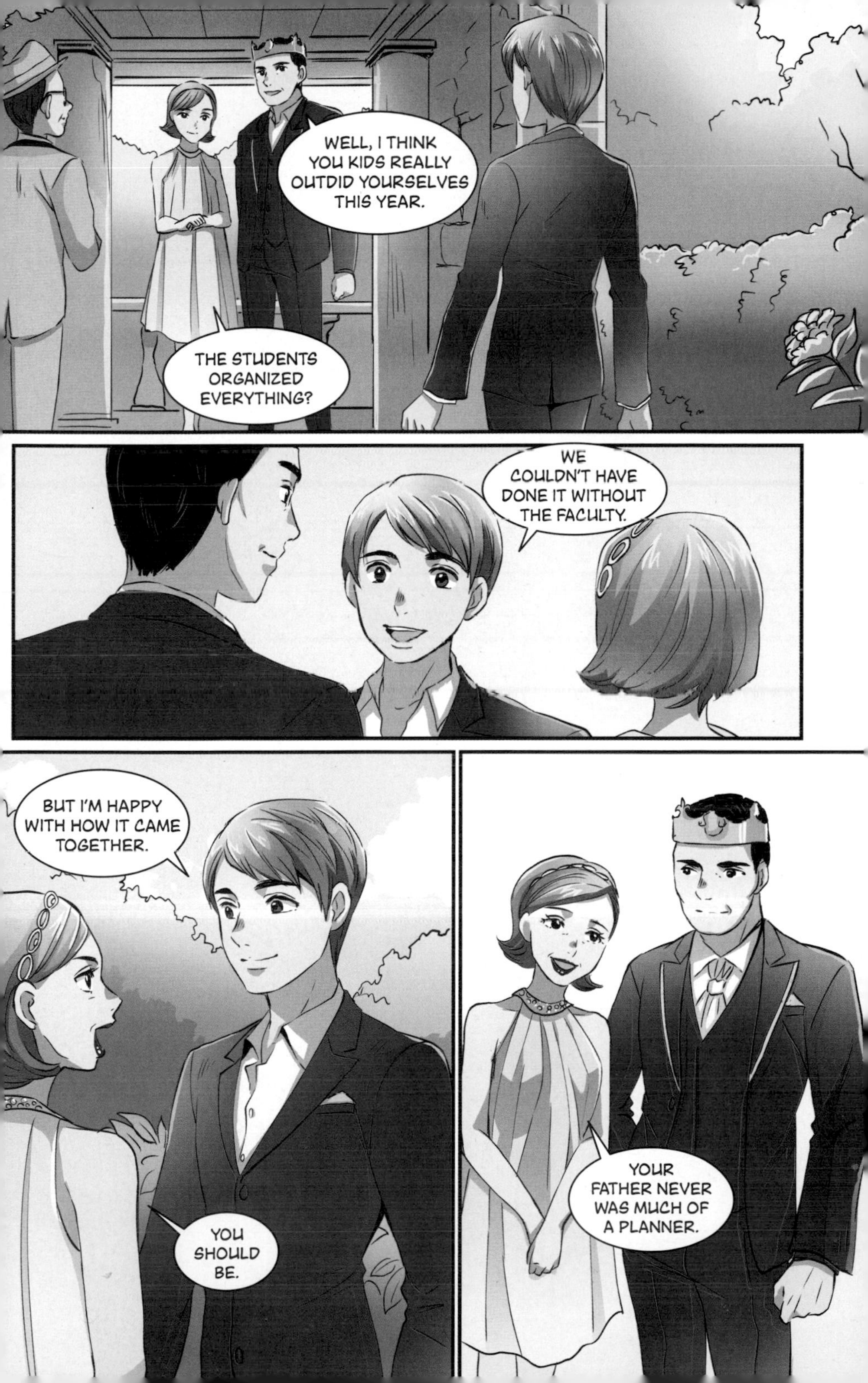
WELL, I THINK YOU KIDS REALLY OUTDID YOURSELVES THIS YEAR.
THE STUDENTS ORGANIZED EVERYTHING?
WE COULDN'T HAVE DONE IT WITHOUT THE FACULTY.
BUT I'M HAPPY WITH HOW IT CAME TOGETHER.
YOU SHOULD BE.
YOUR FATHER NEVER WAS MUCH OF A PLANNER.

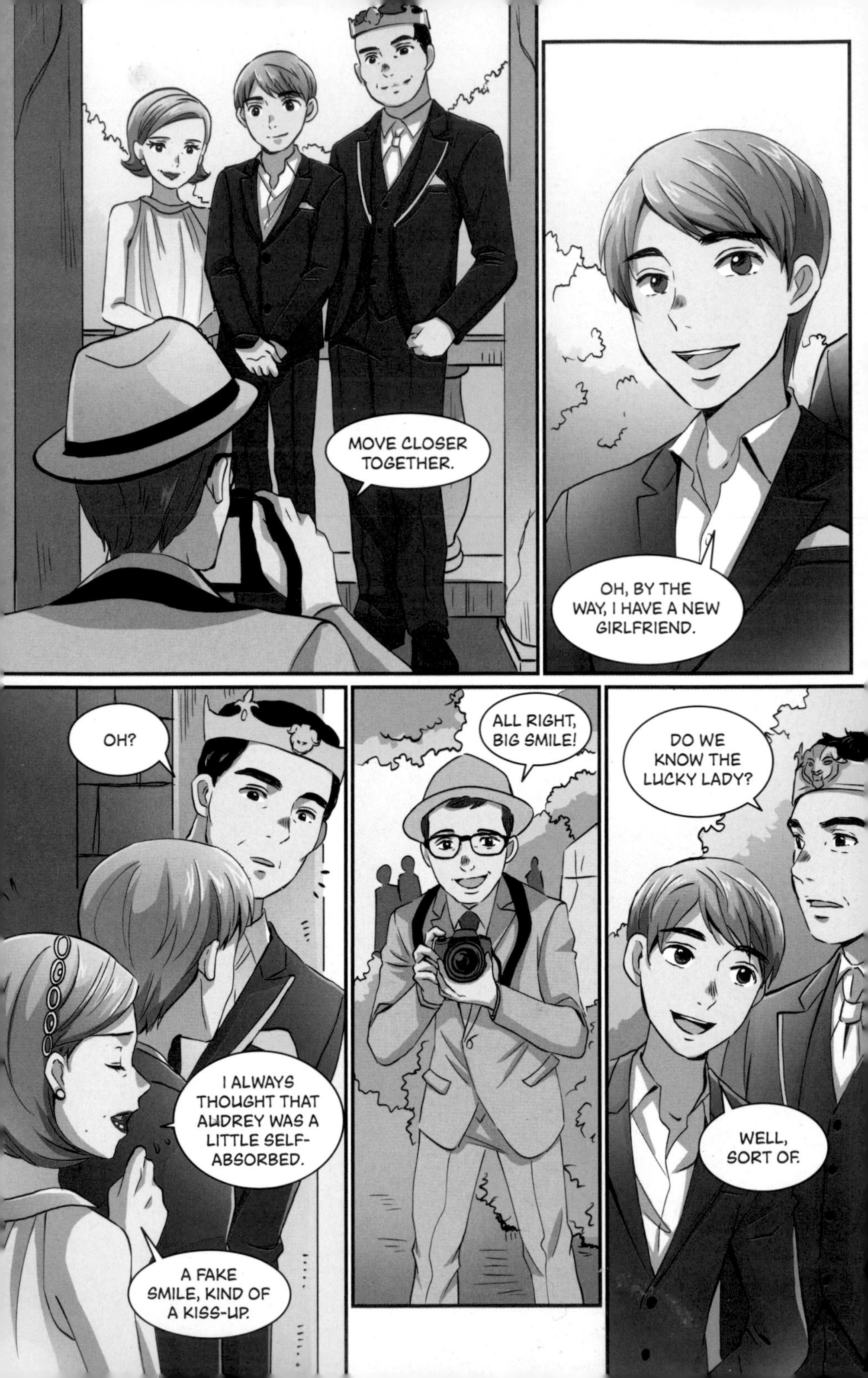
MOVE CLOSER TOGETHER.
OH, BY THE WAY, I HAVE A NEW GIRLFRIEND.
OH?
I ALWAYS THOUGHT THAT AUDREY WAS A LITTLE SELF-ABSORBED.
A FAKE SMILE, KIND OF A KISS-UP.
ALL RIGHT, BIG SMILE!
DO WE KNOW THE LUCKY LADY?
WELL, SORT OF.

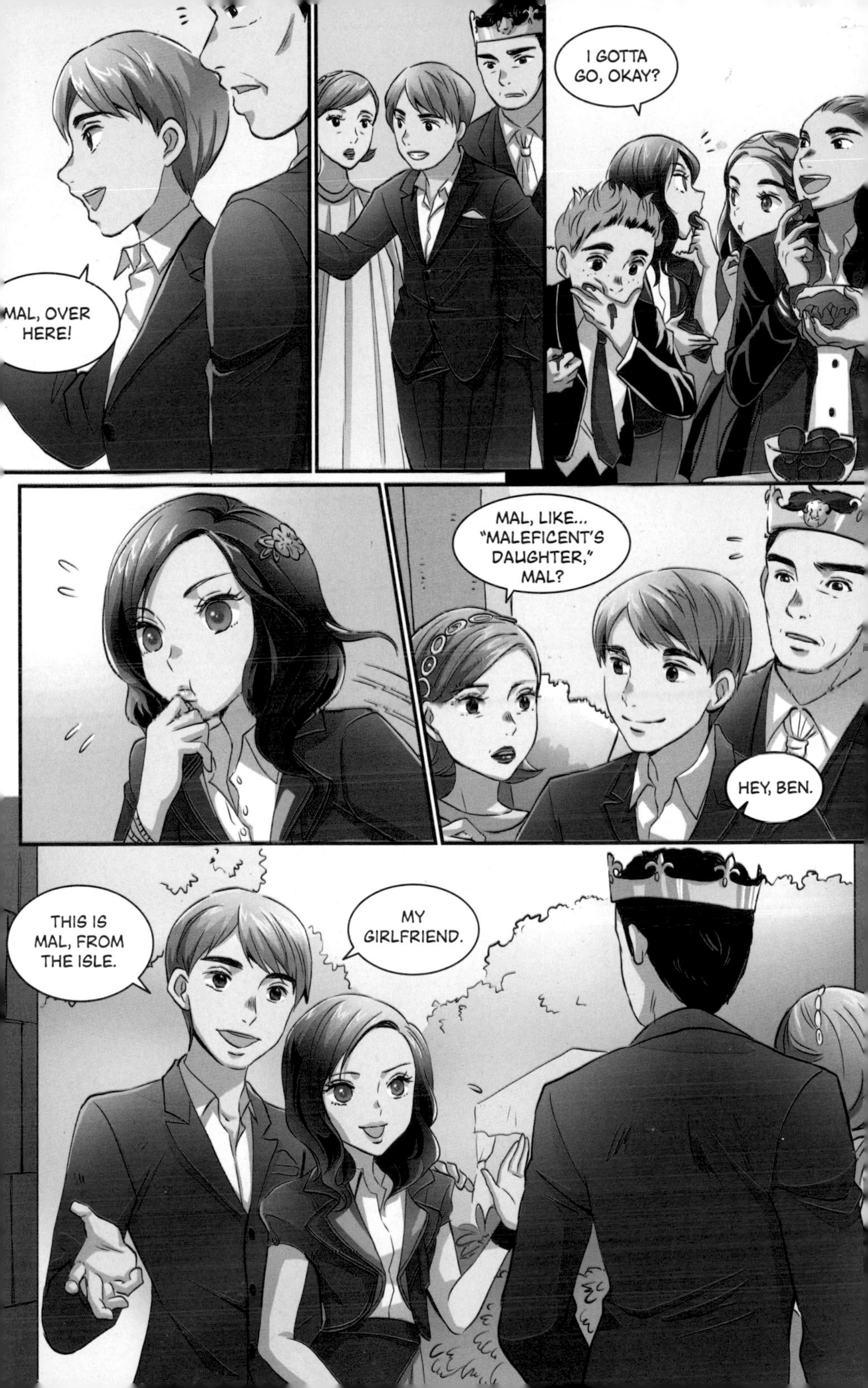
MAL, OVER HERE!
I GOTTA GO, OKAY?
MAL, LIKE... "MALEFICENT'S DAUGHTER," MAL?
HEY, BEN.
THIS IS MAL, FROM THE ISLE.
MY GIRLFRIEND.

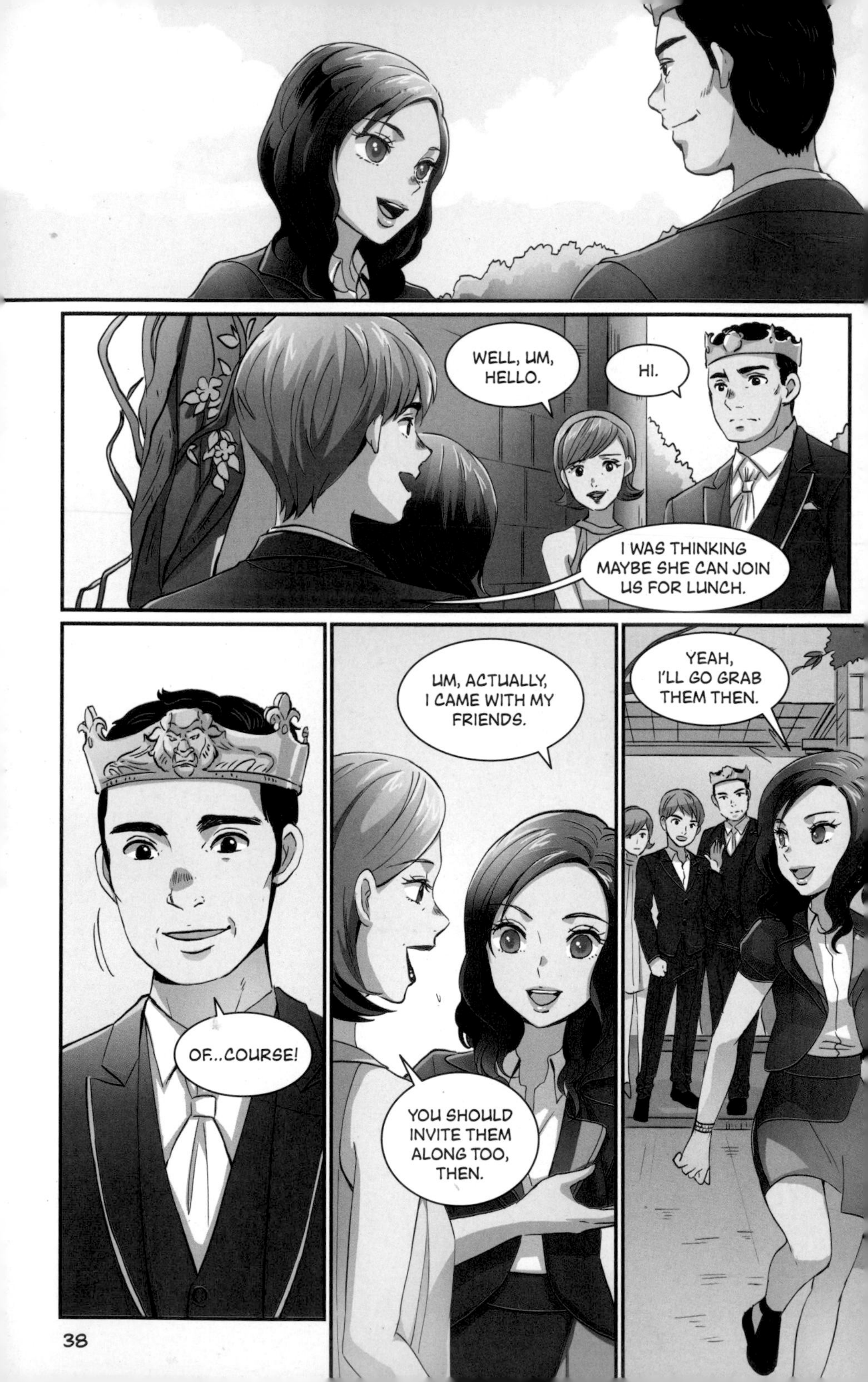
WELL, UM, HELLO.
HI.
I WAS THINKING MAYBE SHE CAN JOIN US FOR LUNCH.
OF...COURSE!
UM, ACTUALLY, I CAME WITH MY FRIENDS.
YOU SHOULD INVITE THEM ALONG TOO, THEN.
YEAH, I'LL GO GRAB THEM THEN.

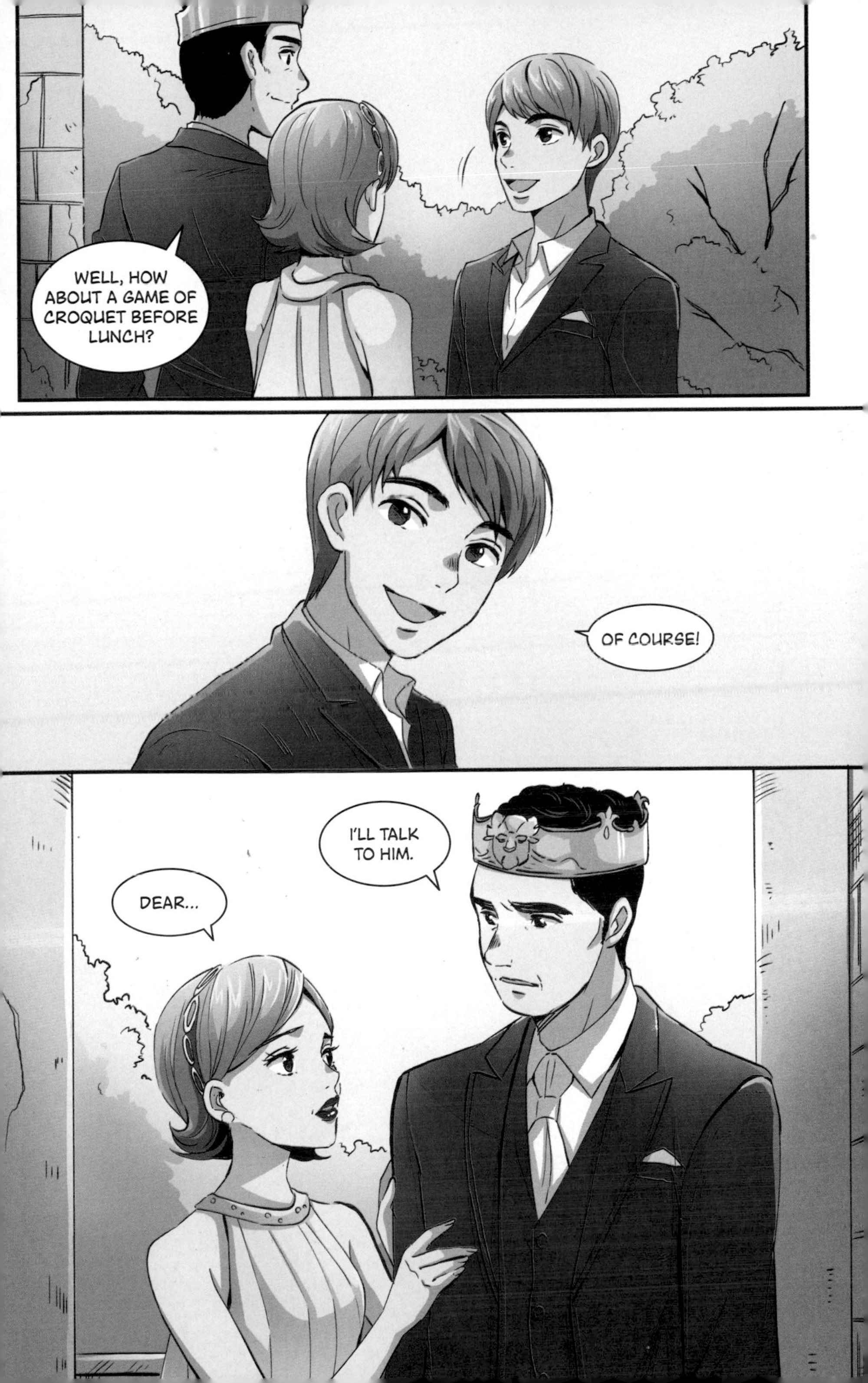
WELL, HOW ABOUT A GAME OF CROQUET BEFORE LUNCH?
OF COURSE!
I'LL TALK TO HIM.
DEAR...

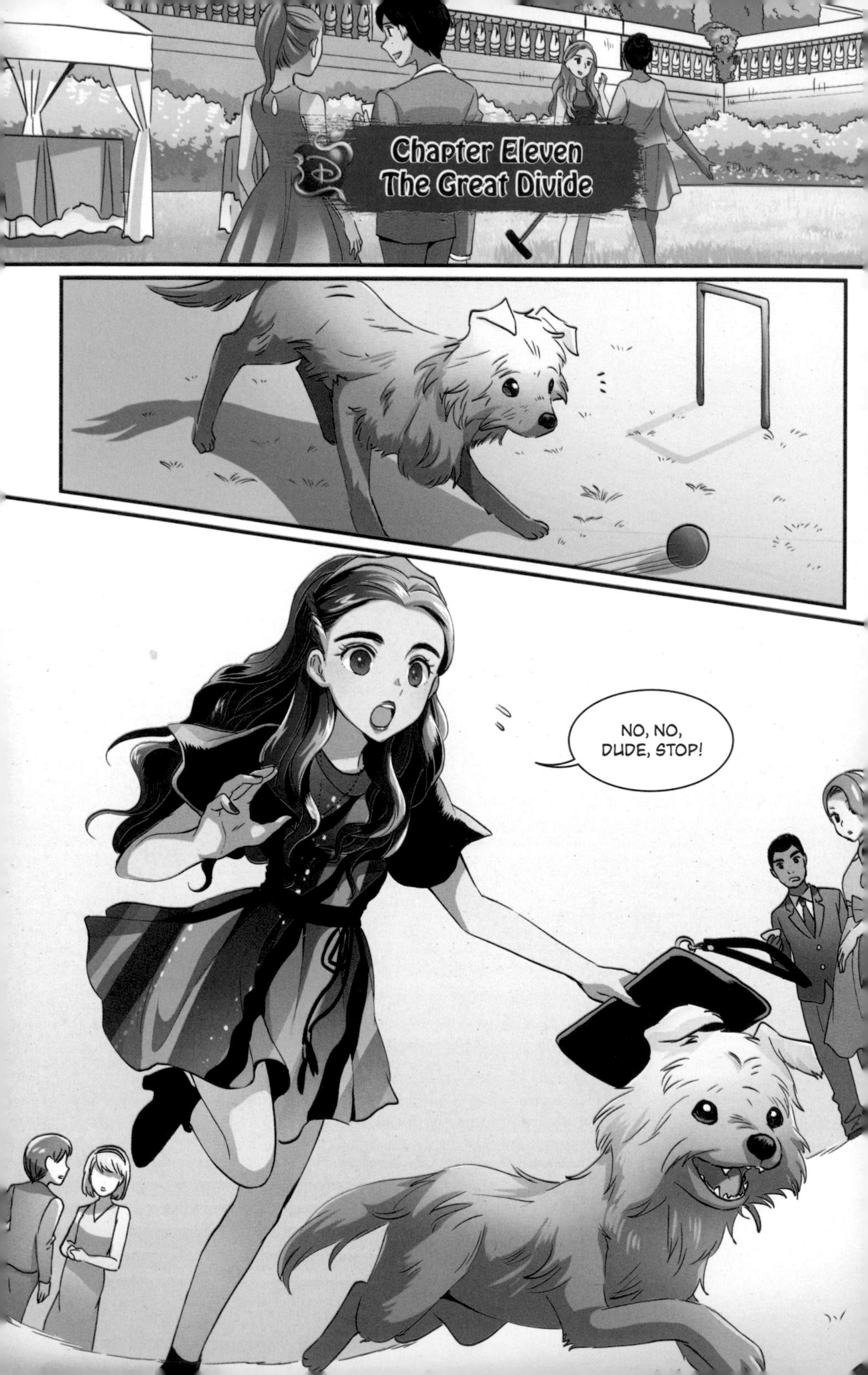
Chapter Eleven
The Great Divide
NO, NO, DUDE, STOP!

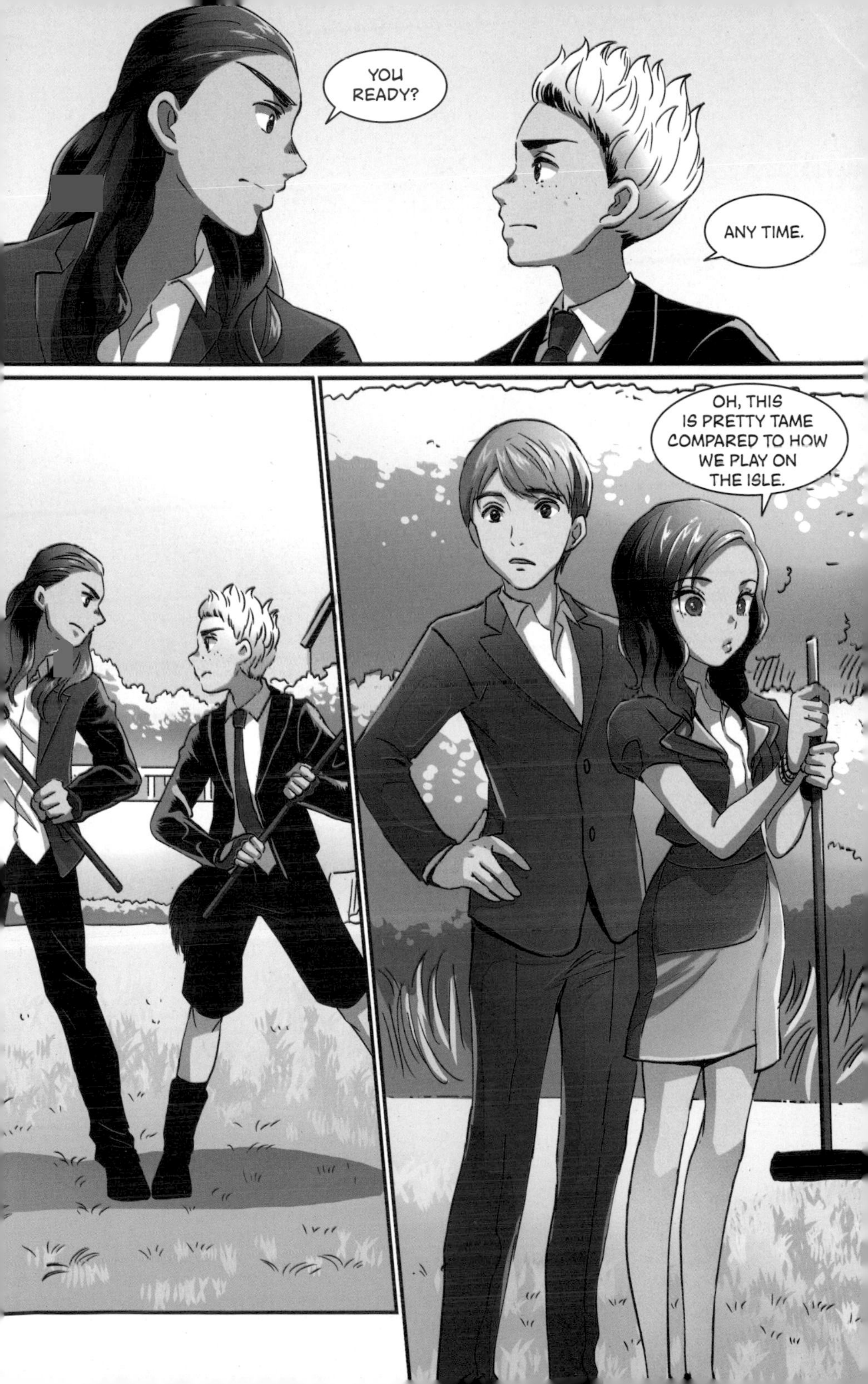
YOU READY?
ANY TIME.
OH, THIS IS PRETTY TAME COMPARED TO HOW WE PLAY ON THE ISLE.

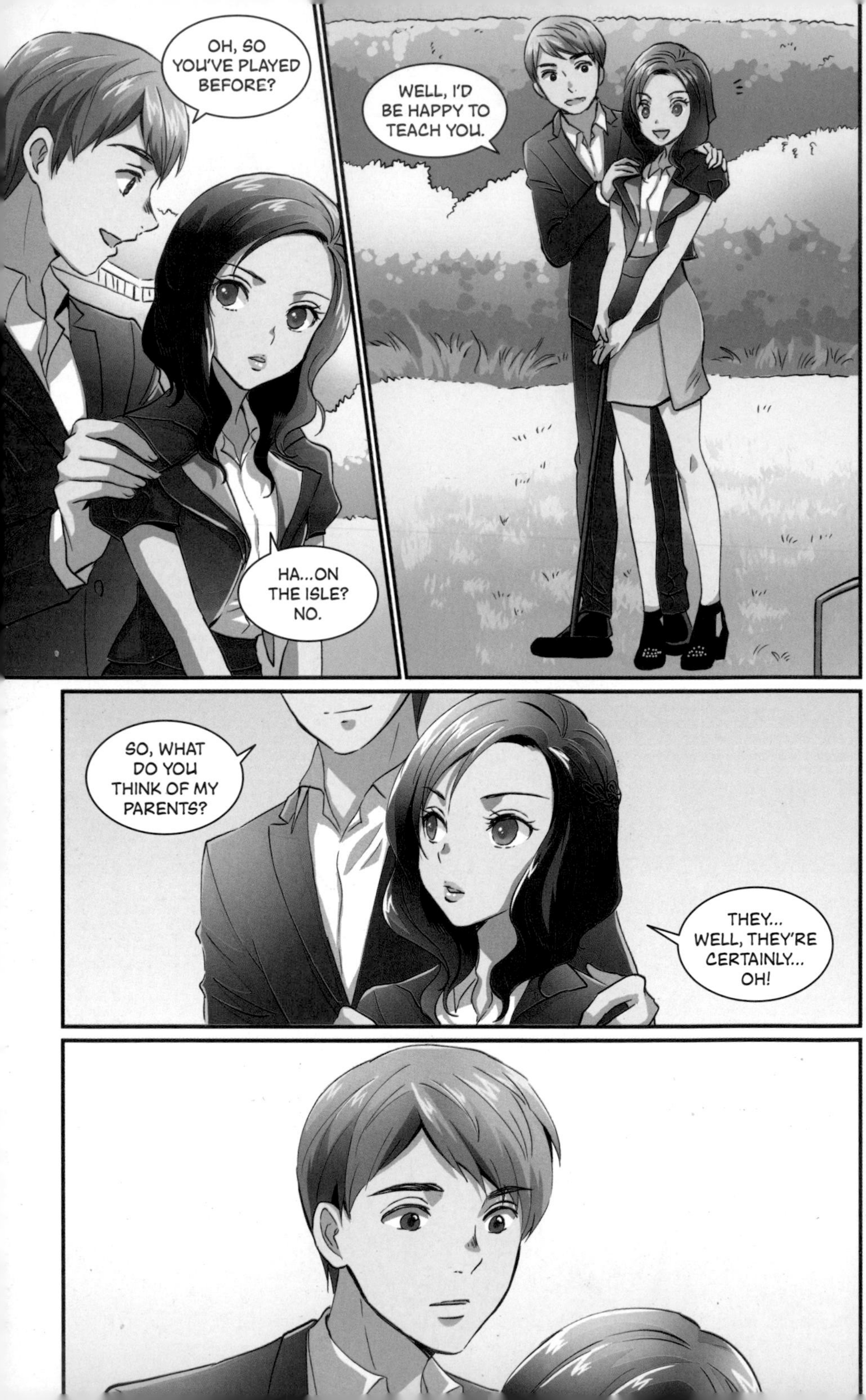
OH, SO YOU'VE PLAYED BEFORE?
HA...ON THE ISLE? NO.
WELL, I'D BE HAPPY TO TEACH YOU.
SO, WHAT DO YOU THINK OF MY PARENTS?
THEY... WELL, THEY'RE CERTAINLY... OH!

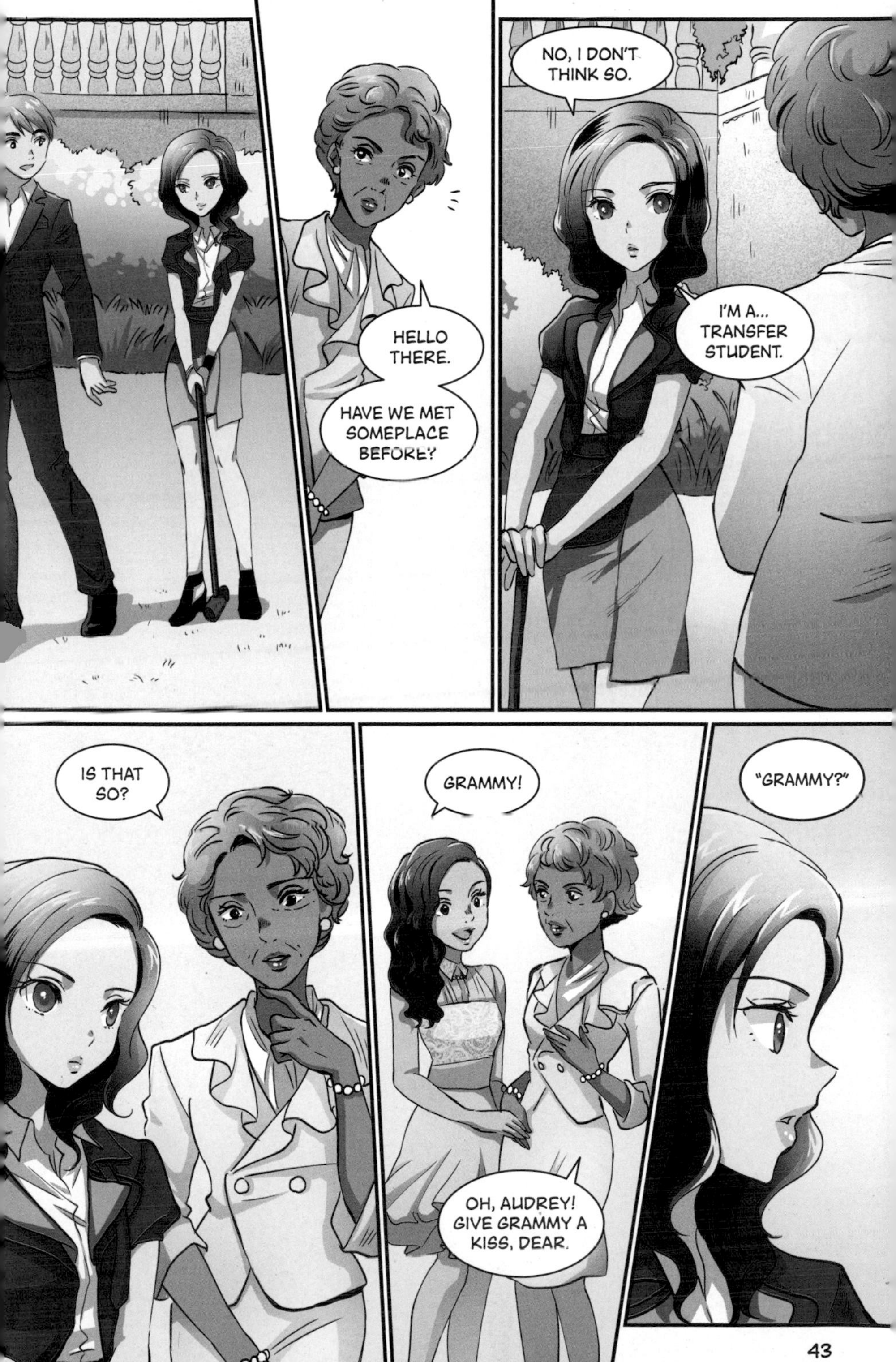
HELLO THERE.
HAVE WE MET SOMEPLACE BEFORE?
NO, I DON'T THINK SO.
I'M A... TRANSFER STUDENT.
IS THAT SO?
GRAMMY!
OH, AUDREY! GIVE GRAMMY A KISS, DEAR.
"GRAMMY?"

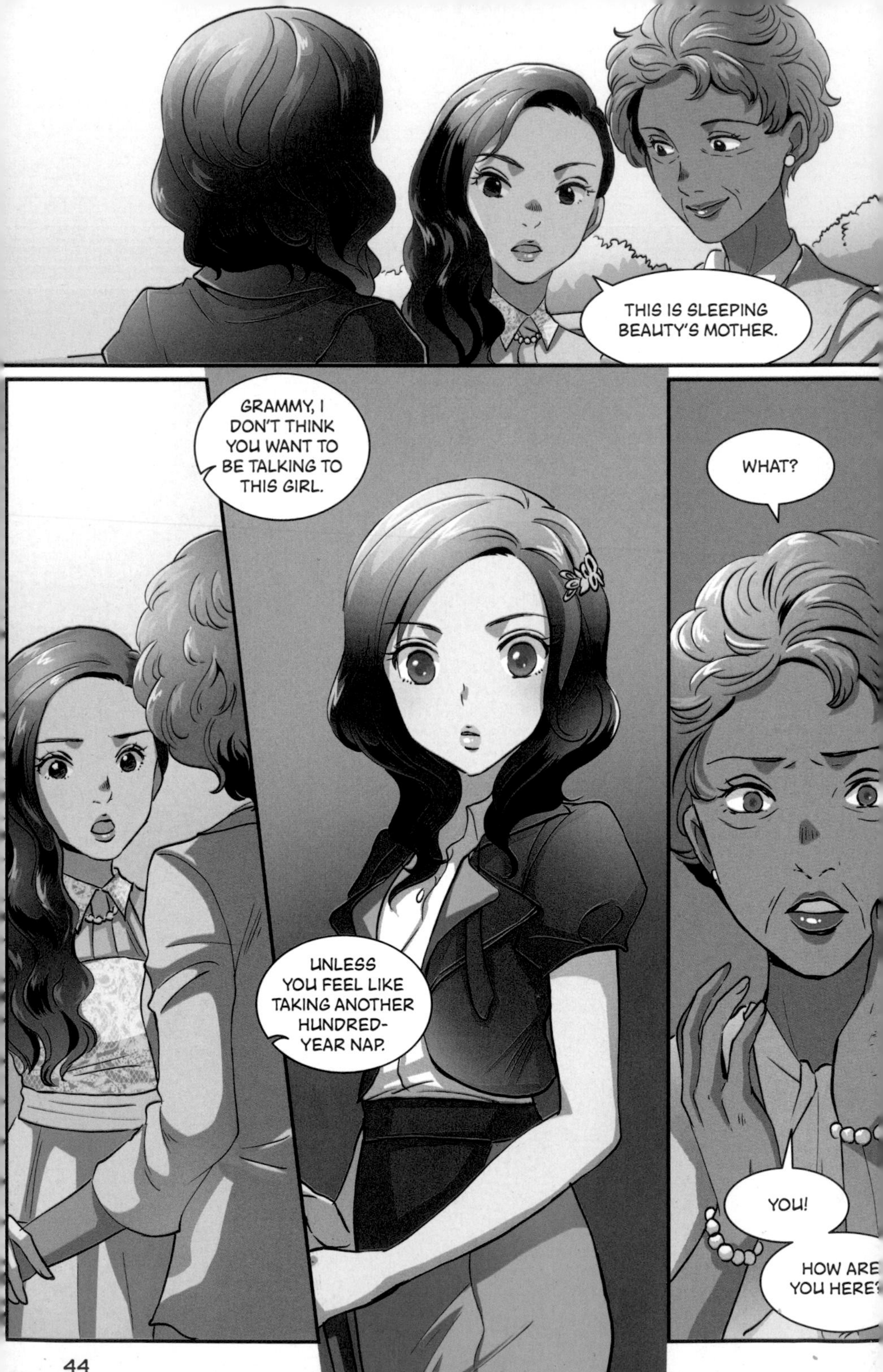
THIS IS SLEEPING BEAUTY'S MOTHER.
GRAMMY, I DON'T THINK YOU WANT TO BE TALKING TO THIS GIRL.
WHAT?
UNLESS YOU FEEL LIKE TAKING ANOTHER HUNDRED-YEAR NAP.
YOU!
HOW ARE YOU HERE?

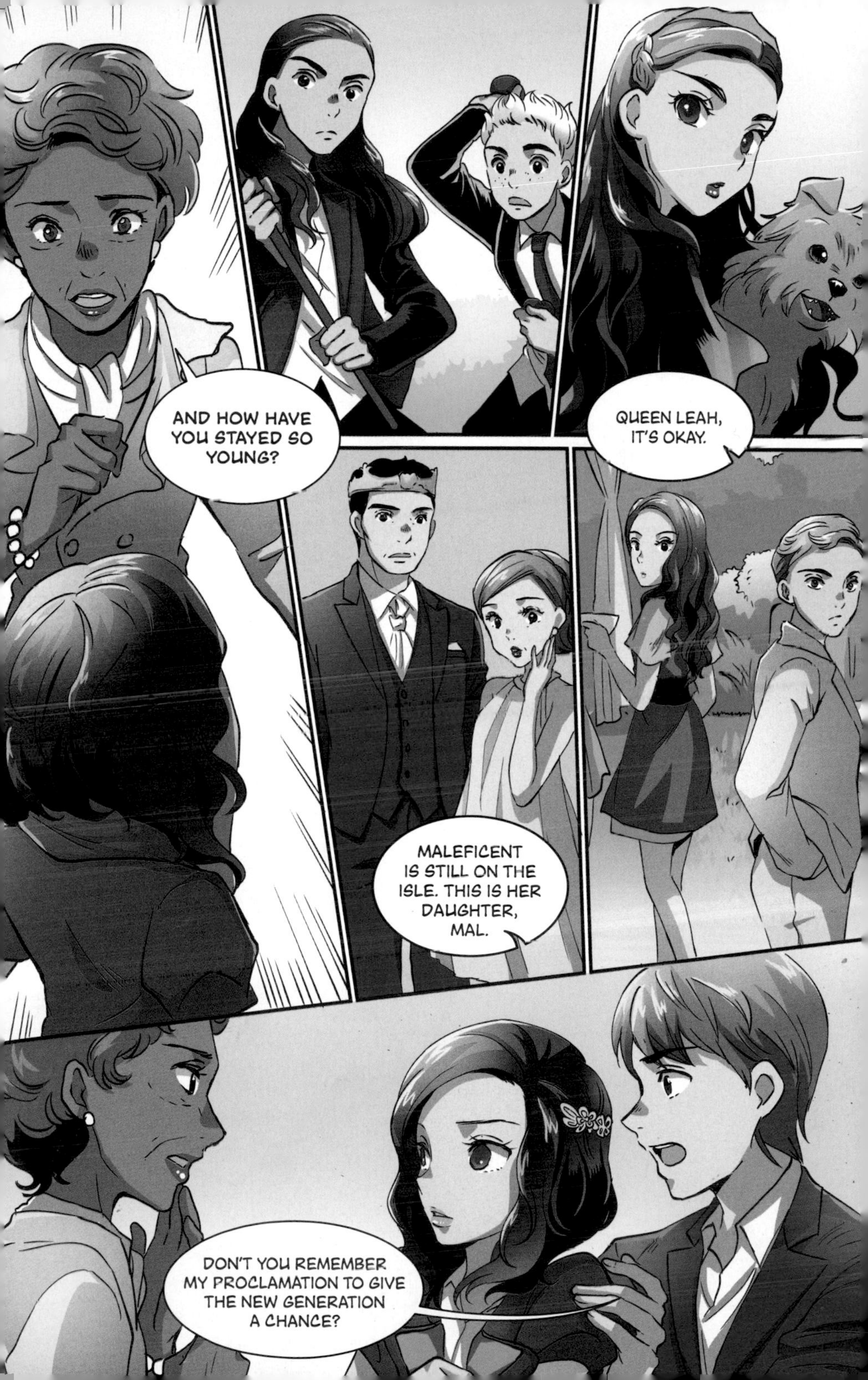
AND HOW HAVE YOU STAYED SO YOUNG?
QUEEN LEAH, IT'S OKAY.
MALEFICENT IS STILL ON THE ISLE. THIS IS HER DAUGHTER, MAL.
DON'T YOU REMEMBER MY PROCLAMATION TO GIVE THE NEW GENERATION A CHANCE?

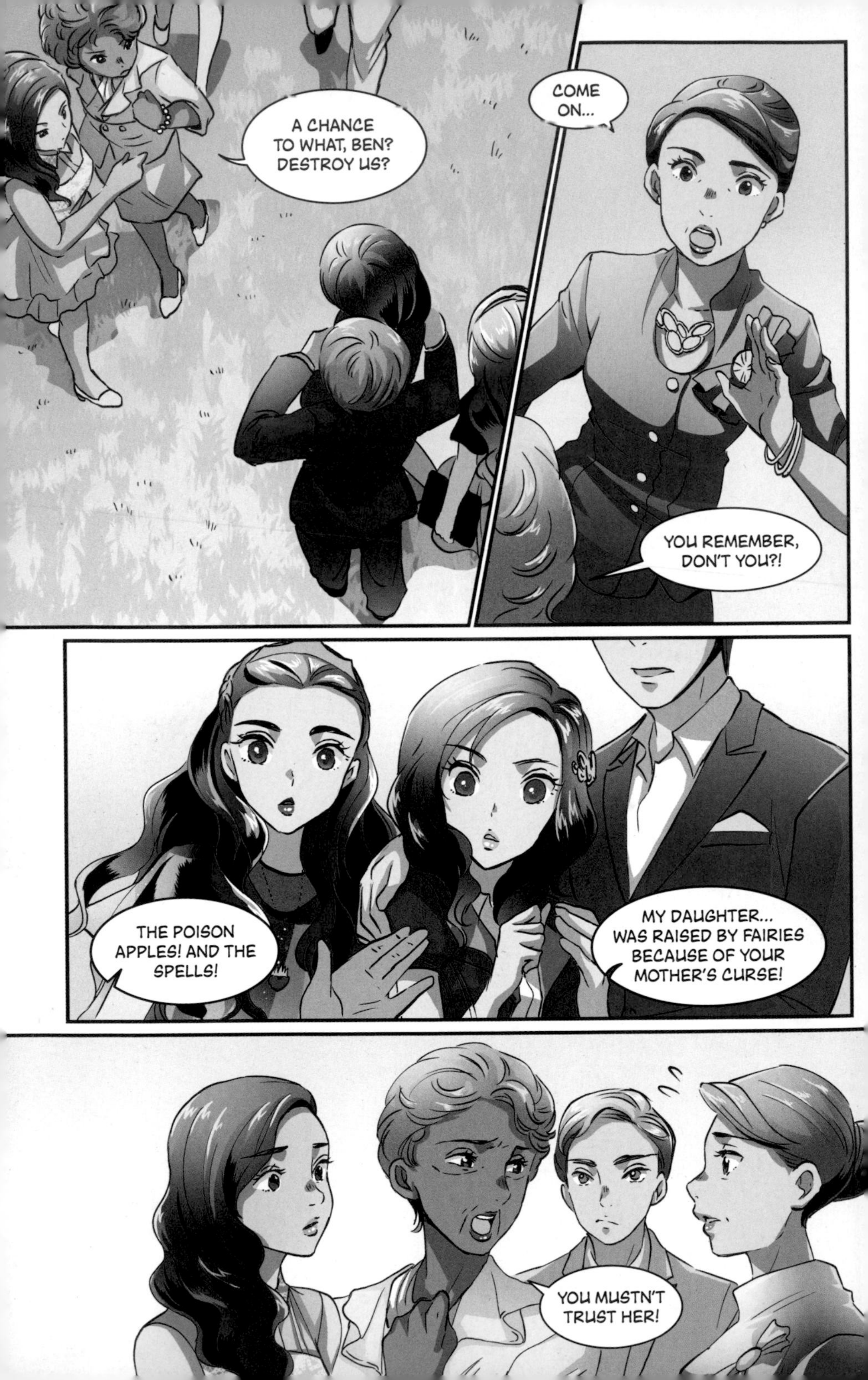
A CHANCE TO WHAT, BEN? DESTROY US?
COME ON...
YOU REMEMBER, DON'T YOU?!
THE POISON APPLES! AND THE SPELLS!
MY DAUGHTER... WAS RAISED BY FAIRIES BECAUSE OF YOUR MOTHER'S CURSE!
YOU MUSTN'T TRUST HER!

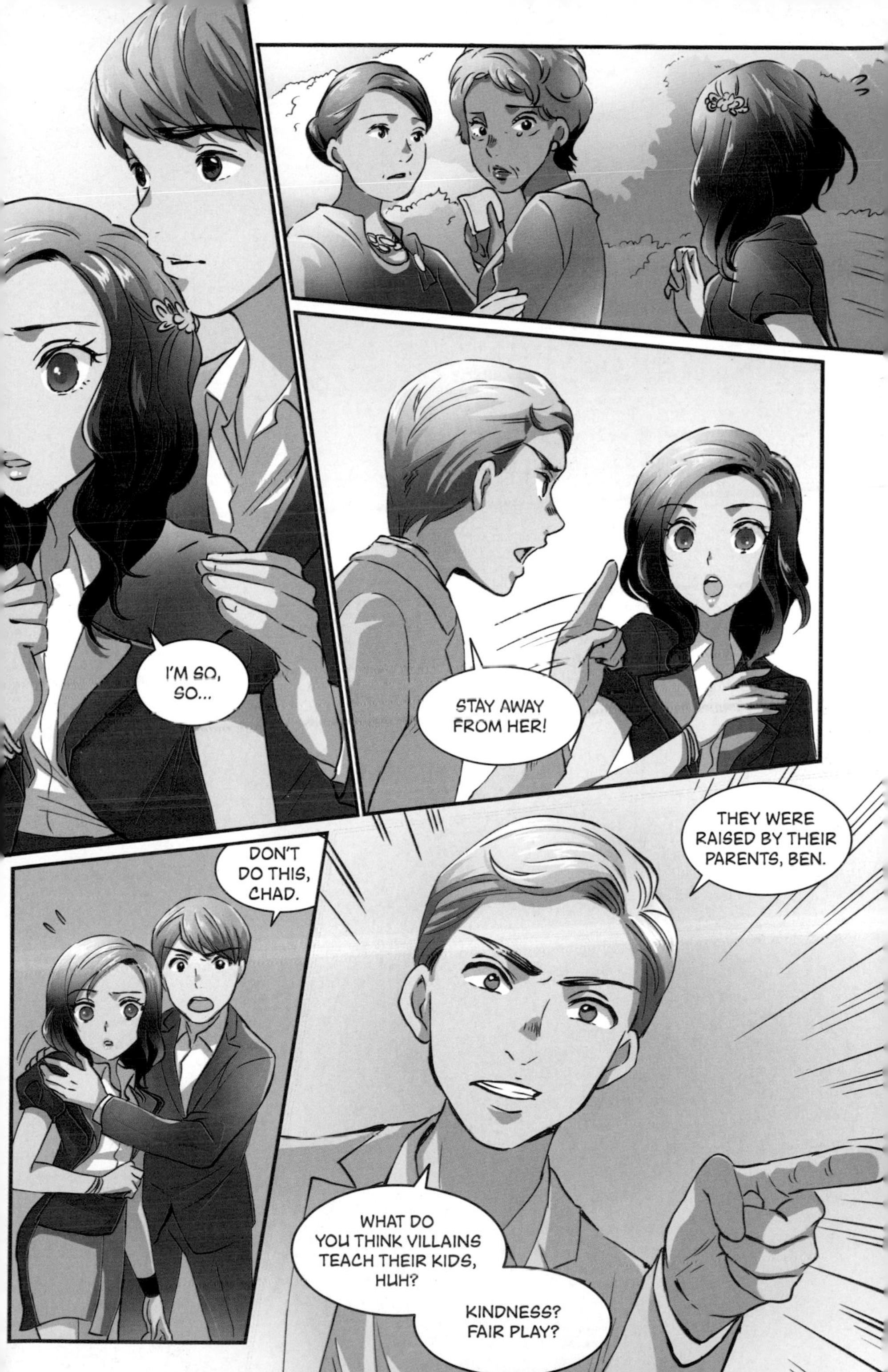
I'M SO, SO...
STAY AWAY FROM HER!
DON'T DO THIS, CHAD.
THEY WERE RAISED BY THEIR PARENTS, BEN.
WHAT DO YOU THINK VILLAINS TEACH THEIR KIDS, HUH?
KINDNESS? FAIR PLAY?

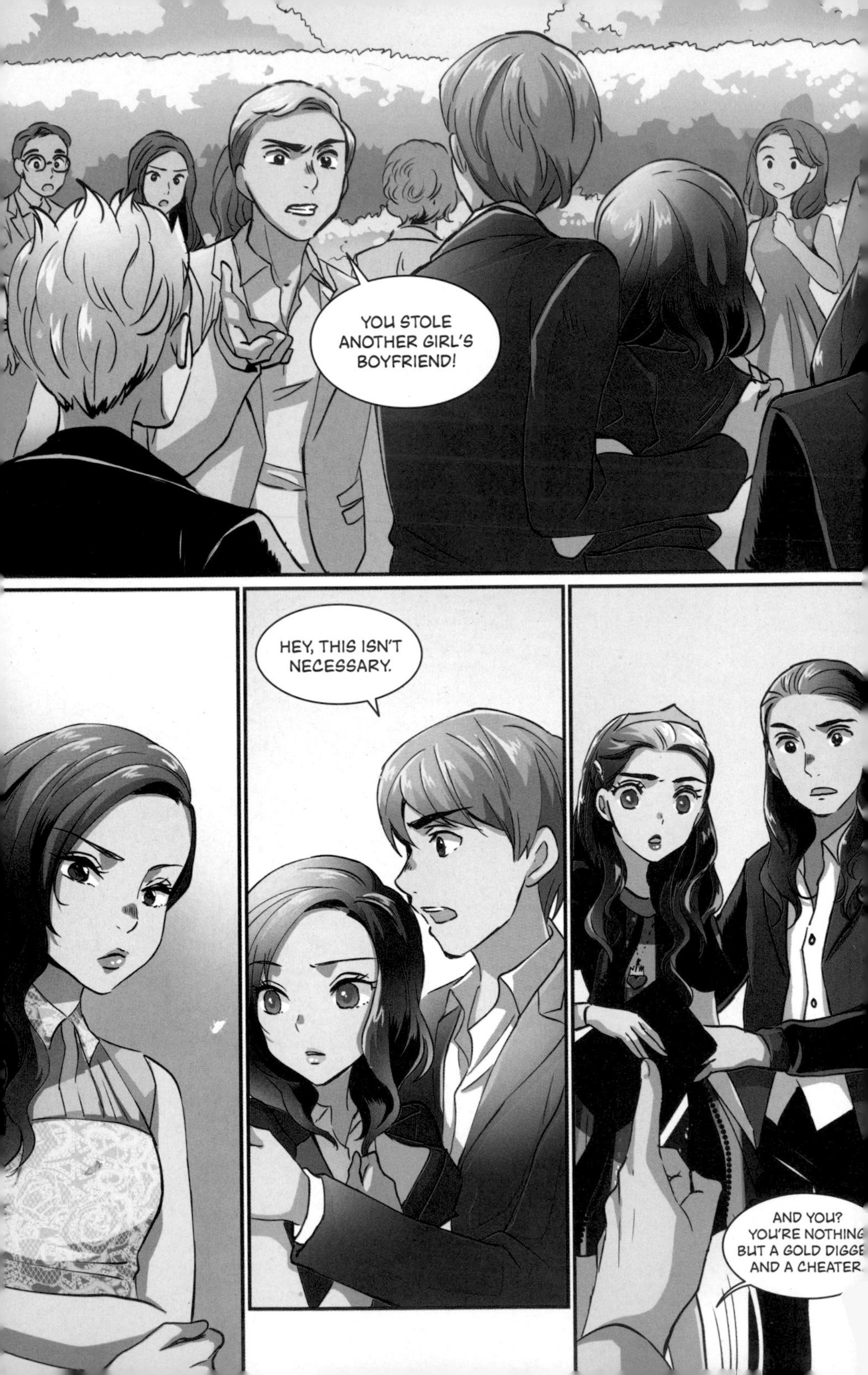
YOU STOLE ANOTHER GIRL'S BOYFRIEND!
HEY, THIS ISN'T NECESSARY.
AND YOU? YOU'RE NOTHING BUT A GOLD DIGGE AND A CHEATER.

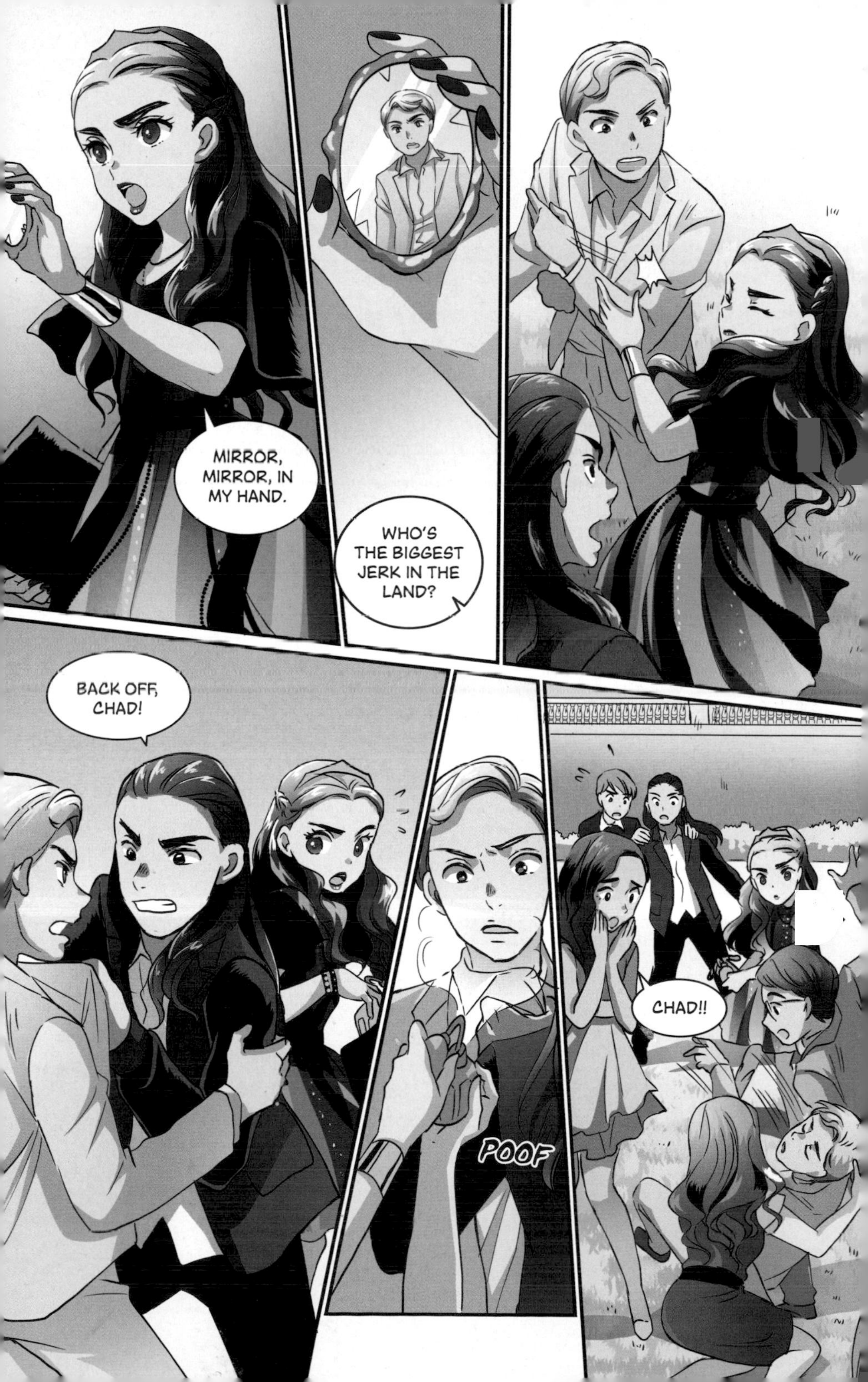
MIRROR, MIRROR, IN MY HAND.
WHO'S THE BIGGEST JERK IN THE LAND?
BACK OFF, CHAD!
POOF
CHAD!!

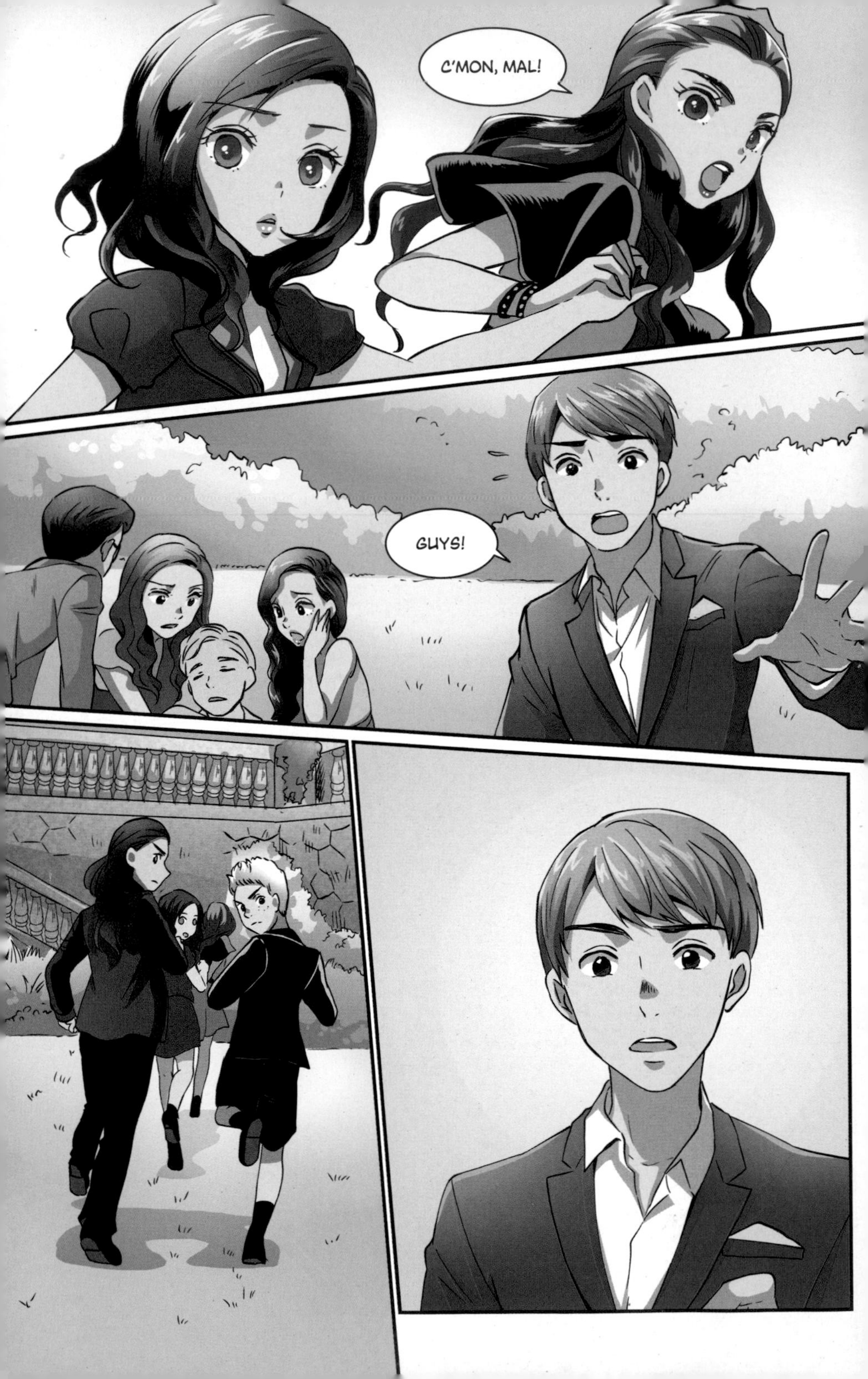
C'MON, MAL!
GUYS!

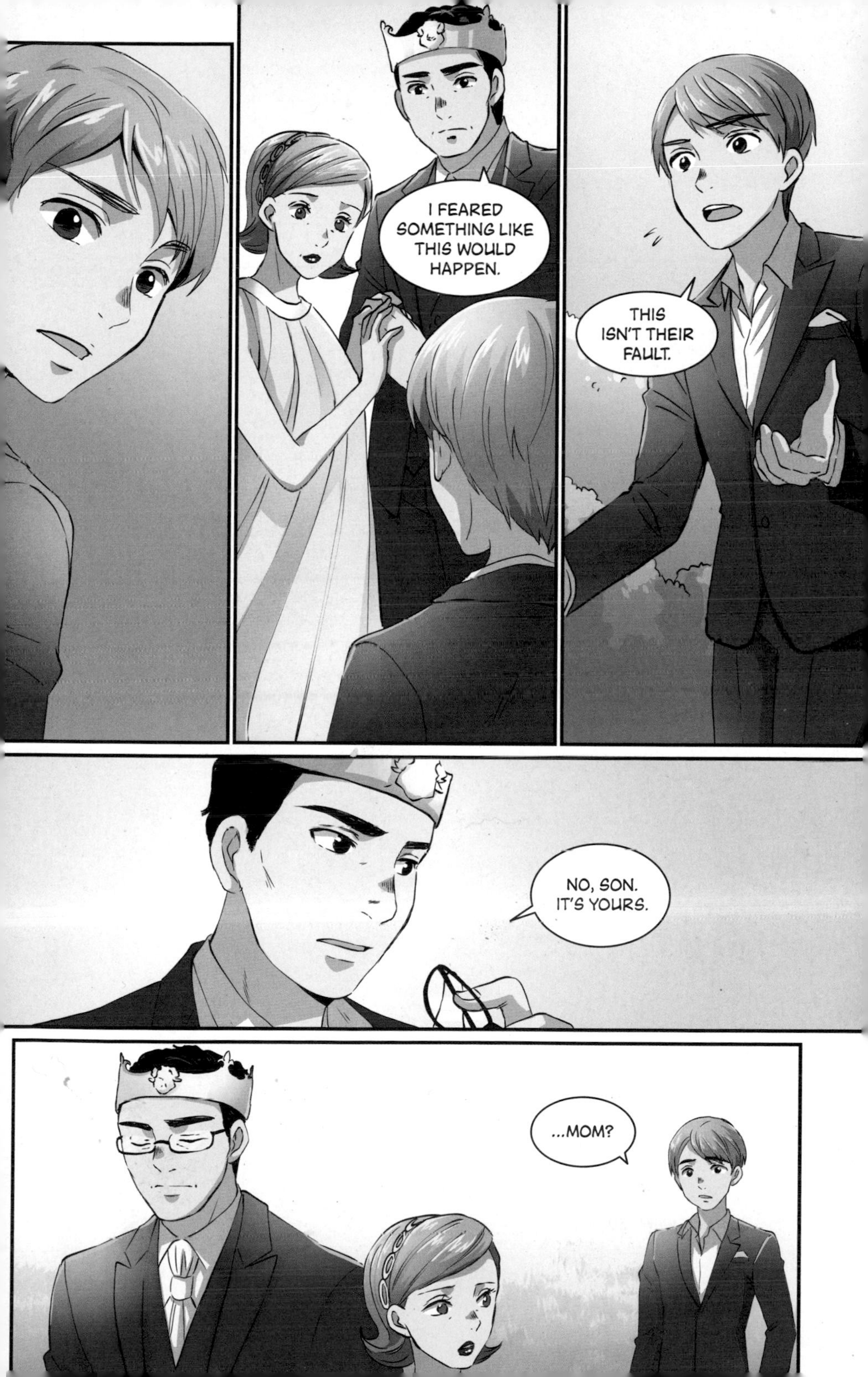
I FEARED SOMETHING LIKE THIS WOULD HAPPEN.
THIS ISN'T THEIR FAULT.
NO, SON. IT'S YOURS.
...MOM?

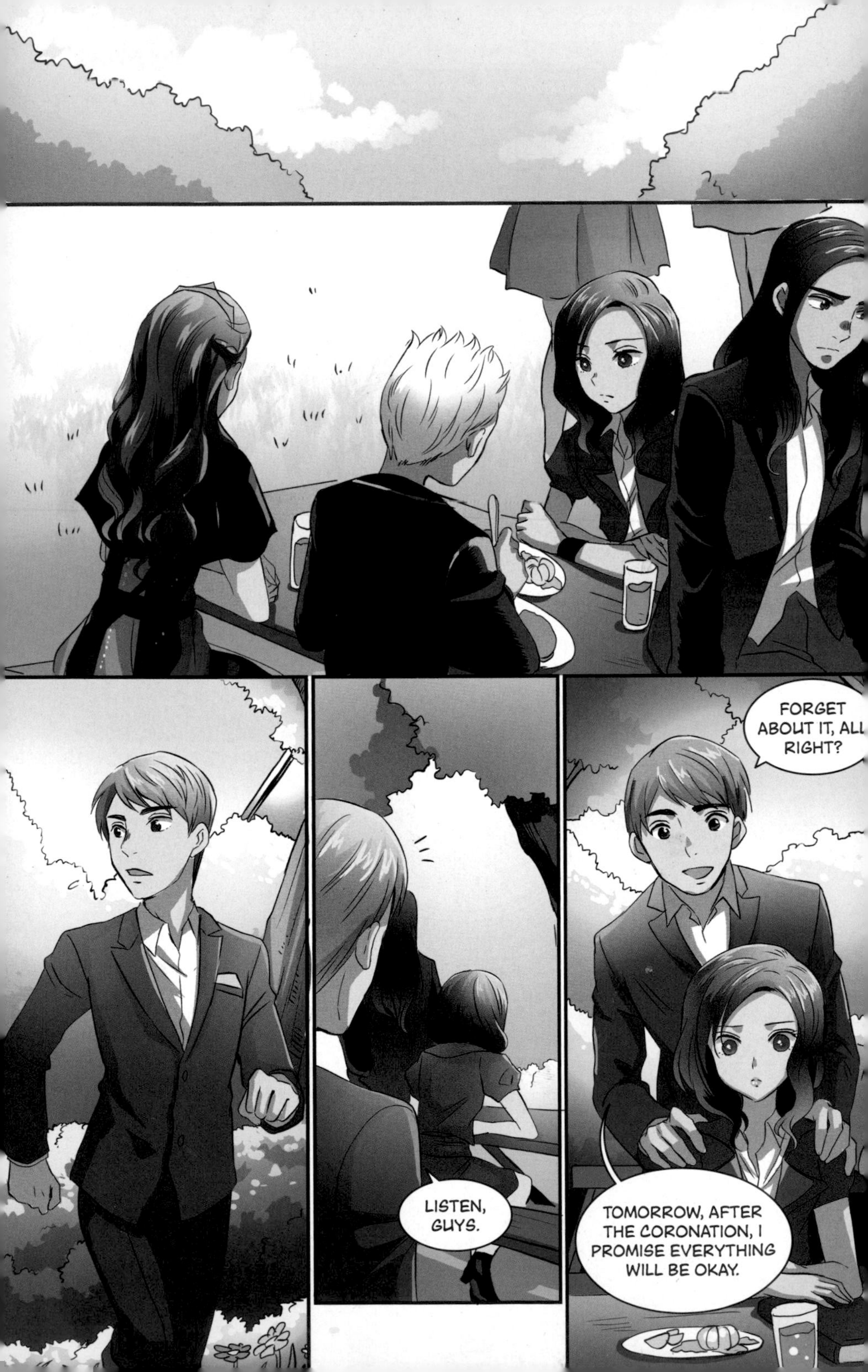
LISTEN, GUYS.
FORGET ABOUT IT, ALL RIGHT?
TOMORROW, AFTER THE CORONATION, I PROMISE EVERYTHING WILL BE OKAY.

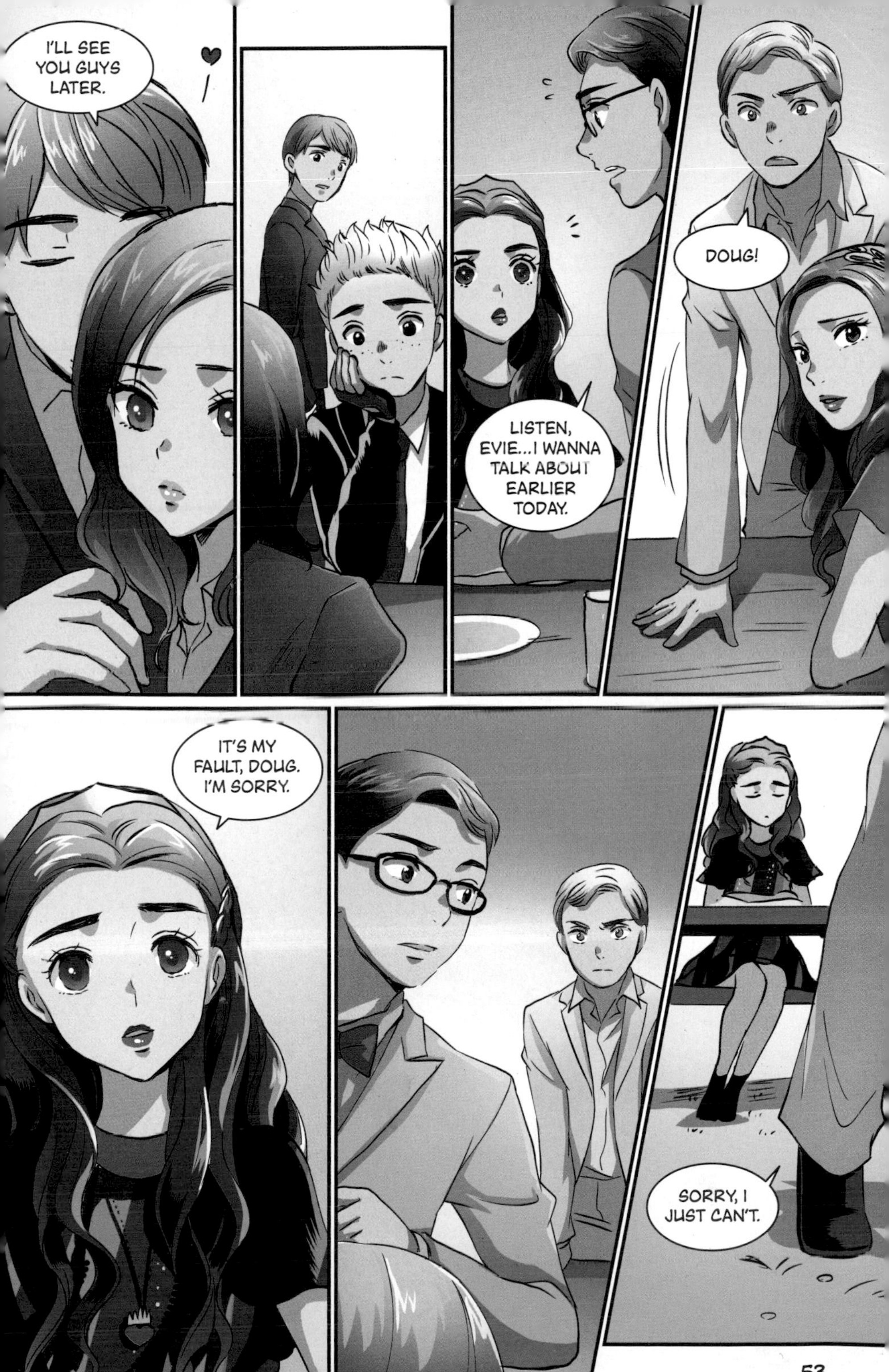
I'LL SEE YOU GUYS LATER.
LISTEN, EVIE...I WANNA TALK ABOUT EARLIER TODAY.
DOUG!
IT'S MY FAULT, DOUG. I'M SORRY.
SORRY, I JUST CAN'T.

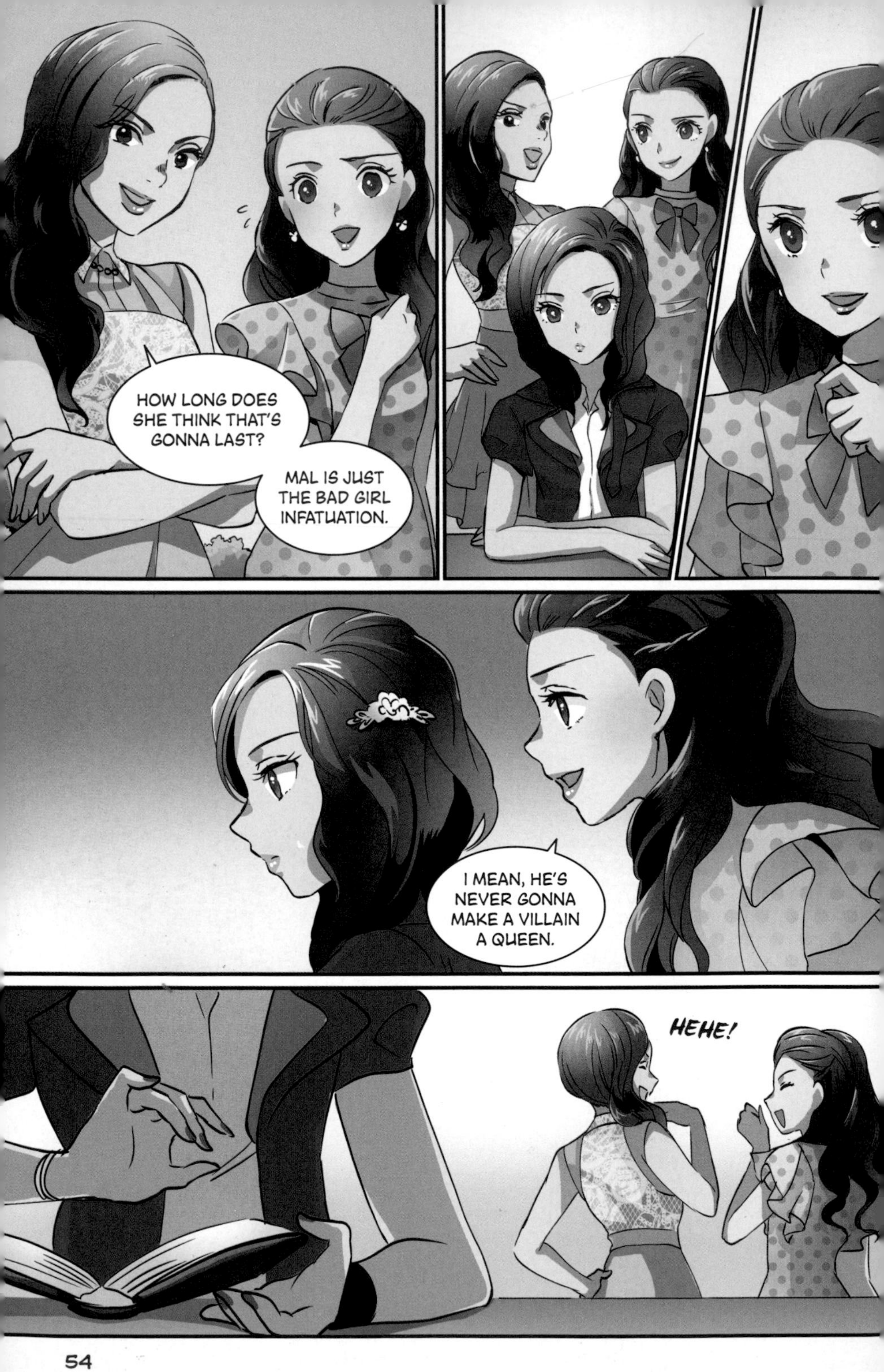
HOW LONG DOES SHE THINK THAT'S GONNA LAST?
MAL IS JUST THE BAD GIRL INFATUATION.
I MEAN, HE'S NEVER GONNA MAKE A VILLAIN A QUEEN.
HEHE!

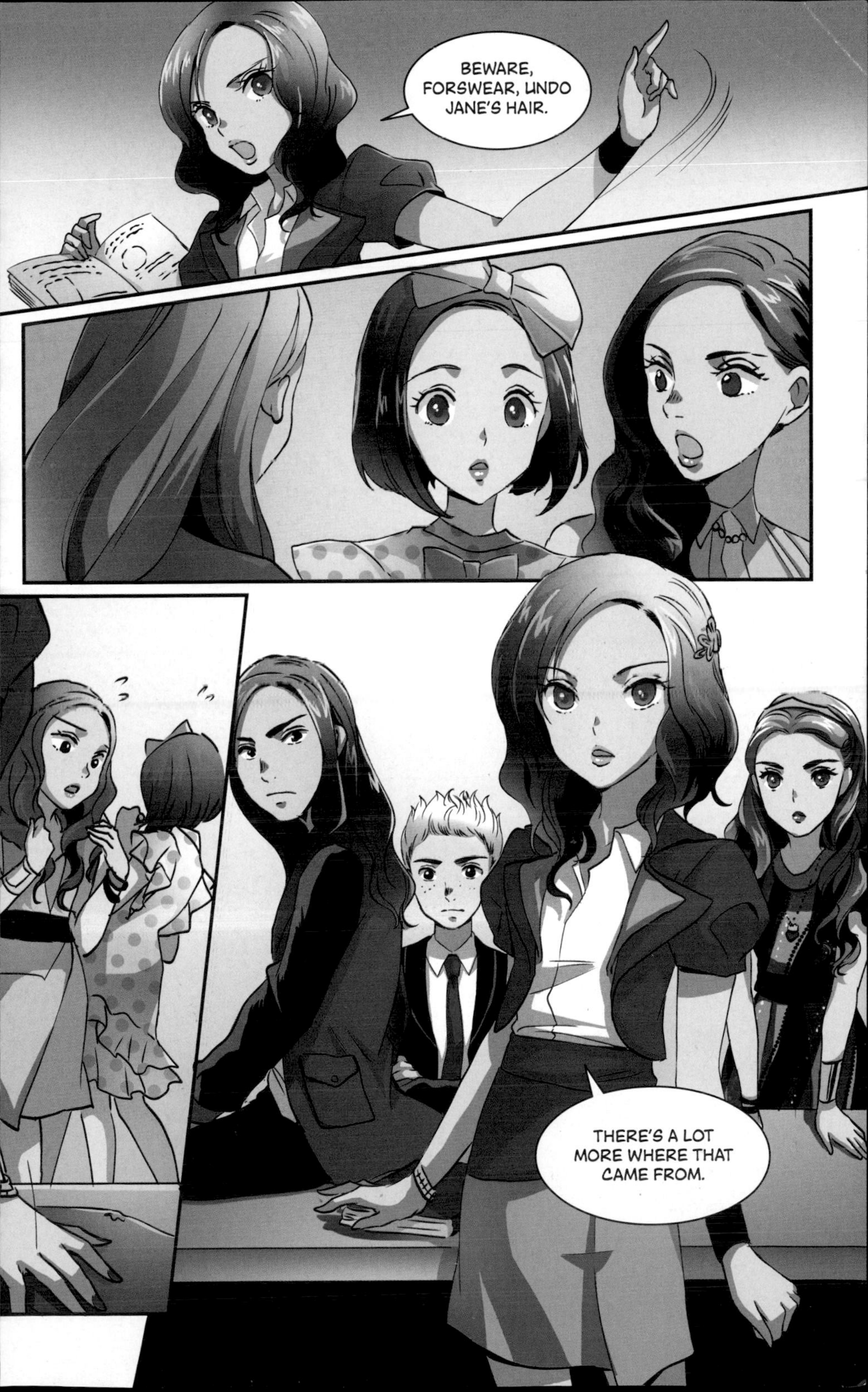
BEWARE, FORSWEAR, UNDO JANE'S HAIR.
THERE'S A LOT MORE WHERE THAT CAME FROM.

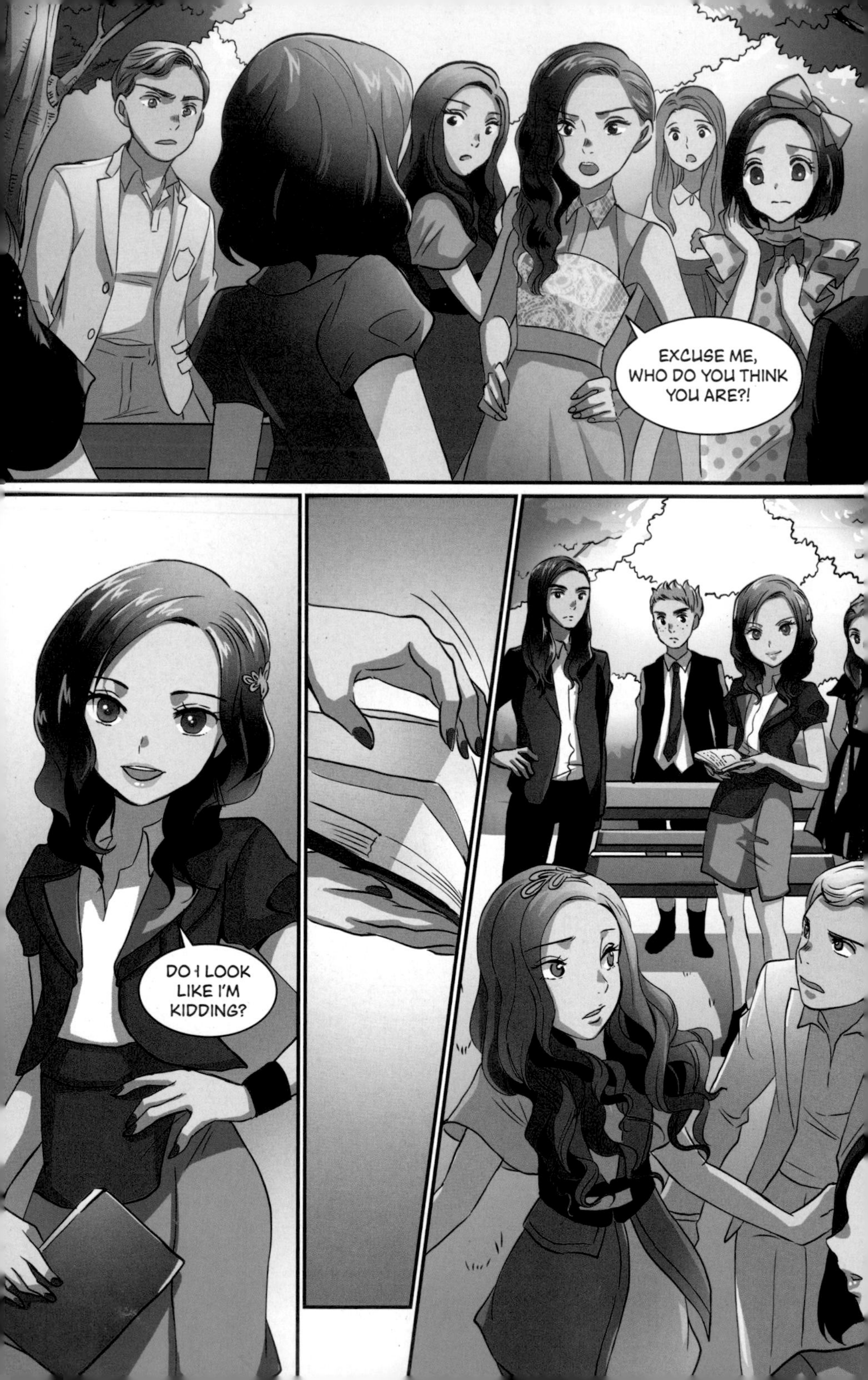
EXCUSE ME, WHO DO YOU THINK YOU ARE?!
DO I LOOK LIKE I'M KIDDING?

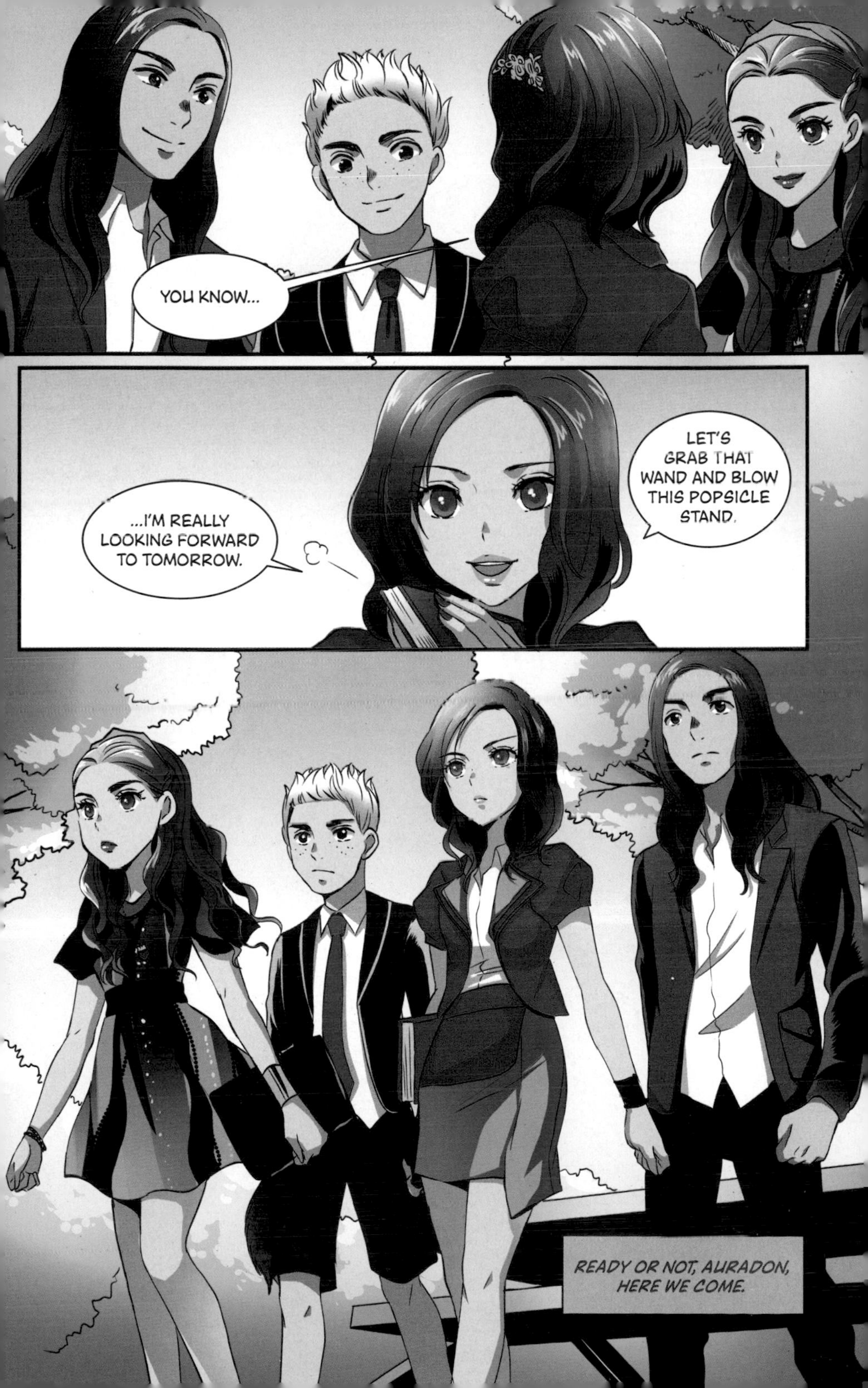
YOU KNOW...
...I'M REALLY LOOKING FORWARD TO TOMORROW.
LET'S GRAB THAT WAND AND BLOW THIS POPSICLE STAND.
READY OR NOT, AURADON, HERE WE COME.

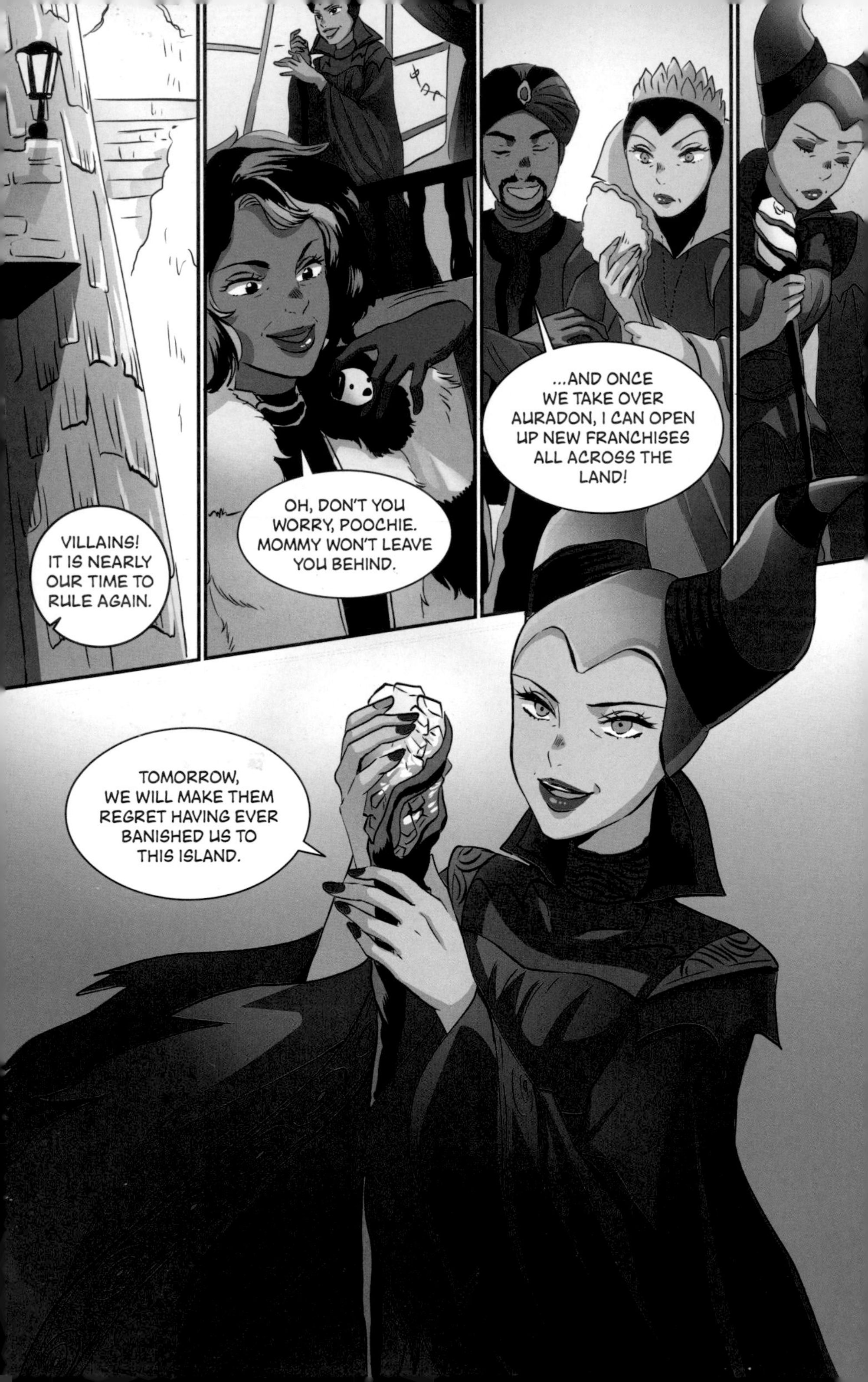
VILLAINS! IT IS NEARLY OUR TIME TO RULE AGAIN.
OH, DON'T YOU WORRY, POOCHIE. MOMMY WON'T LEAVE YOU BEHIND.
...AND ONCE WE TAKE OVER AURADON, I CAN OPEN UP NEW FRANCHISES ALL ACROSS THE LAND!
TOMORROW, WE WILL MAKE THEM REGRET HAVING EVER BANISHED US TO THIS ISLAND.

Chapter Twelve
Change of Heart

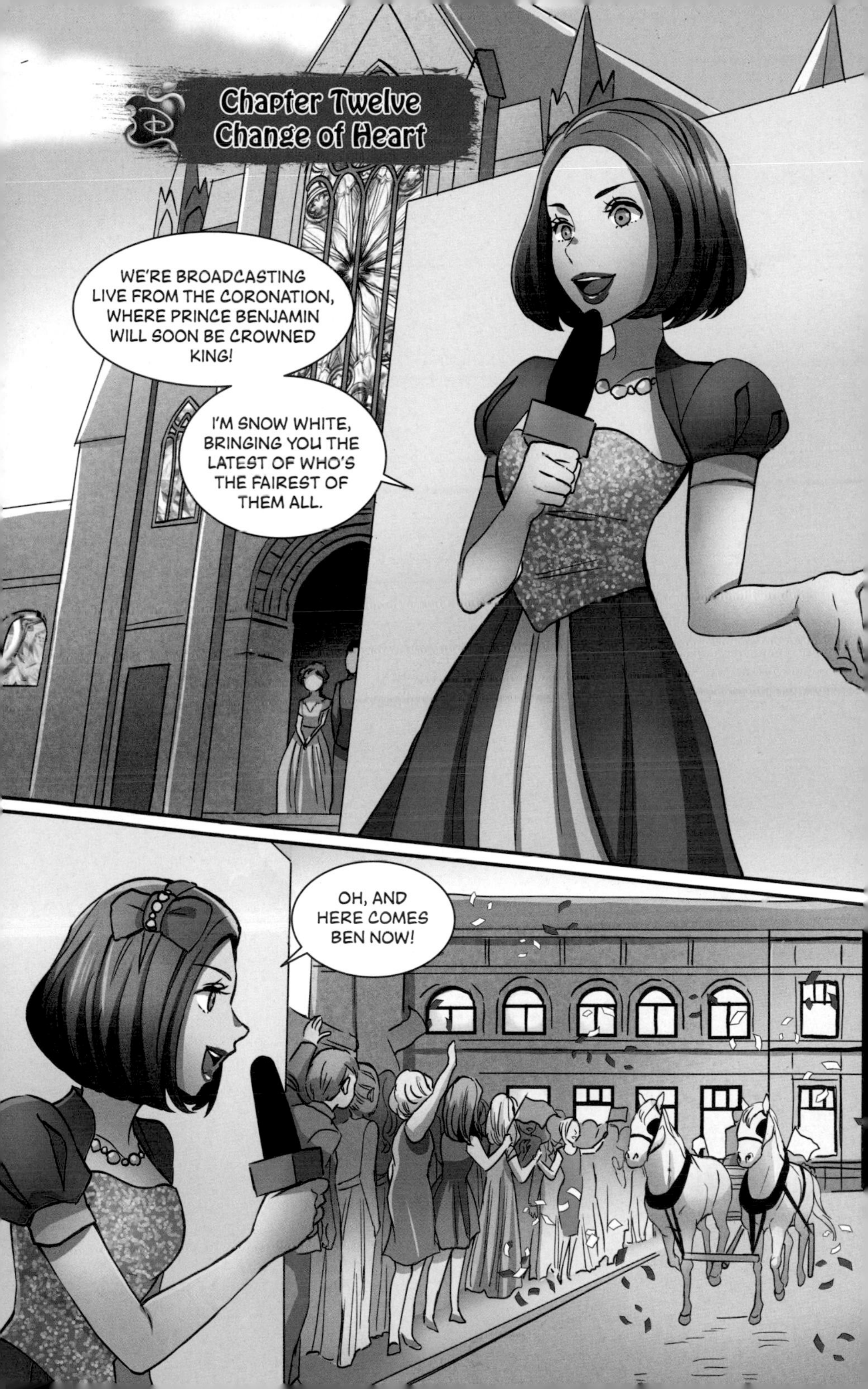
WE'RE BROADCASTING LIVE FROM THE CORONATION, WHERE PRINCE BENJAMIN WILL SOON BE CROWNED KING!
I'M SNOW WHITE, BRINGING YOU THE LATEST OF WHO'S THE FAIREST OF THEM ALL.
OH, AND HERE COMES BEN NOW!

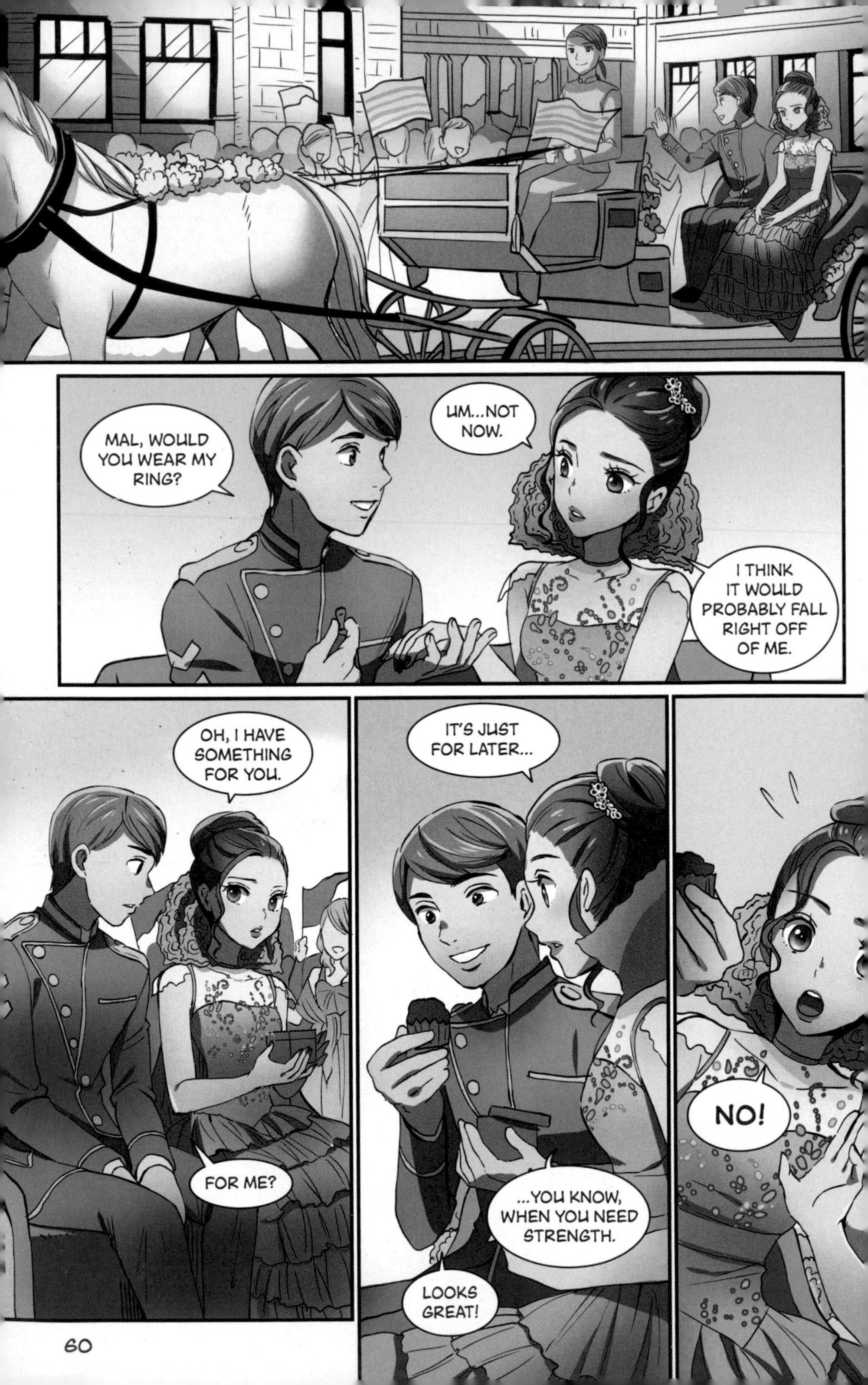
MAL, WOULD YOU WEAR MY RING?
UM...NOT NOW.
I THINK IT WOULD PROBABLY FALL RIGHT OFF OF ME.
OH, I HAVE SOMETHING FOR YOU.
FOR ME?
IT'S JUST FOR LATER...
...YOU KNOW, WHEN YOU NEED STRENGTH.
LOOKS GREAT!
NO!

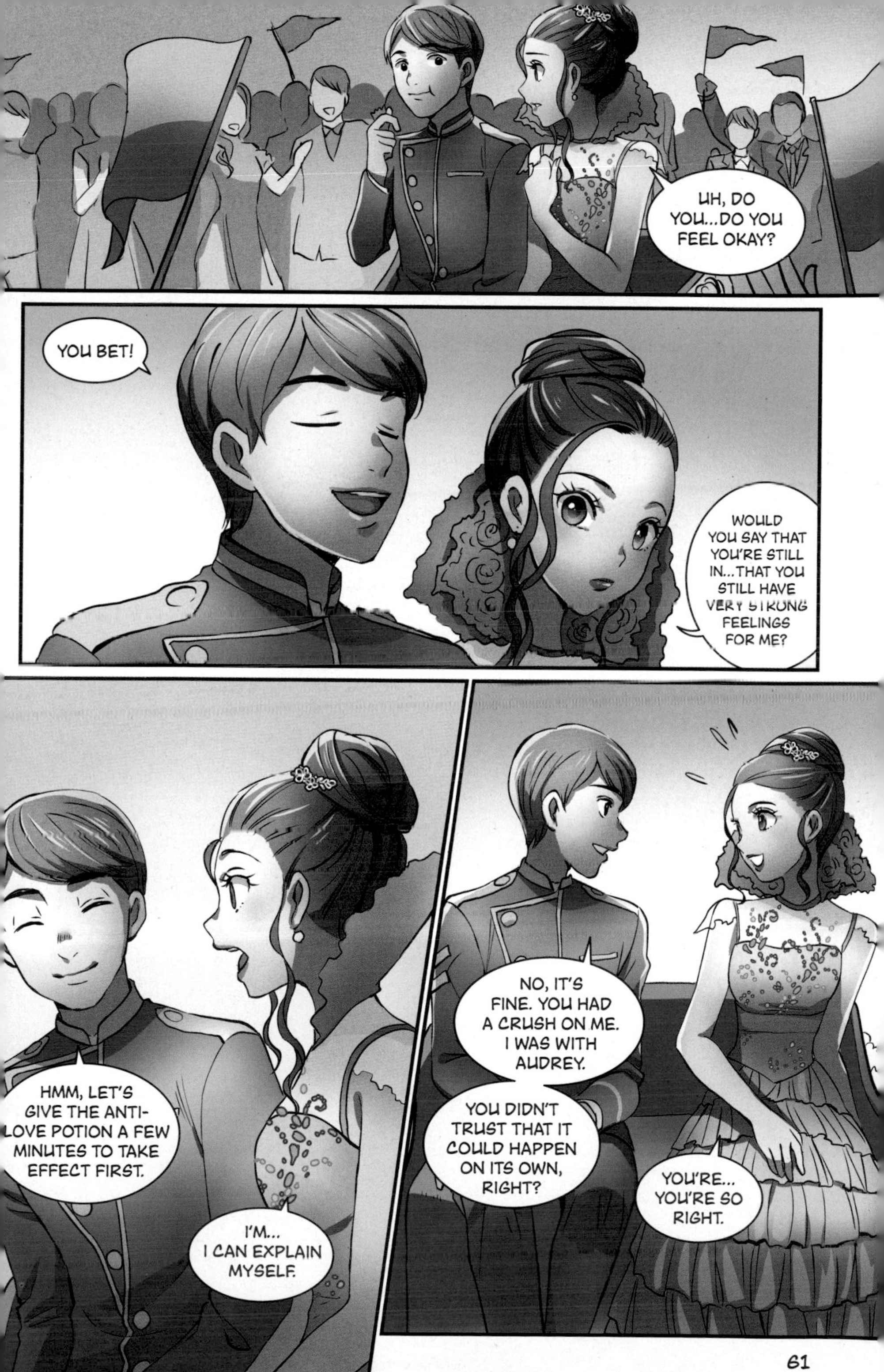
UH, DO YOU...DO YOU FEEL OKAY?
WOULD YOU SAY THAT YOU'RE STILL IN...THAT YOU STILL HAVE VERY STRONG FEELINGS FOR ME?
YOU BET!
HMM, LET'S GIVE THE ANTI-LOVE POTION A FEW MINUTES TO TAKE EFFECT FIRST.
I'M... I CAN EXPLAIN MYSELF.
NO, IT'S FINE. YOU HAD A CRUSH ON ME. I WAS WITH AUDREY.
YOU DIDN'T TRUST THAT IT COULD HAPPEN ON ITS OWN, RIGHT?
YOU'RE... YOU'RE SO RIGHT.

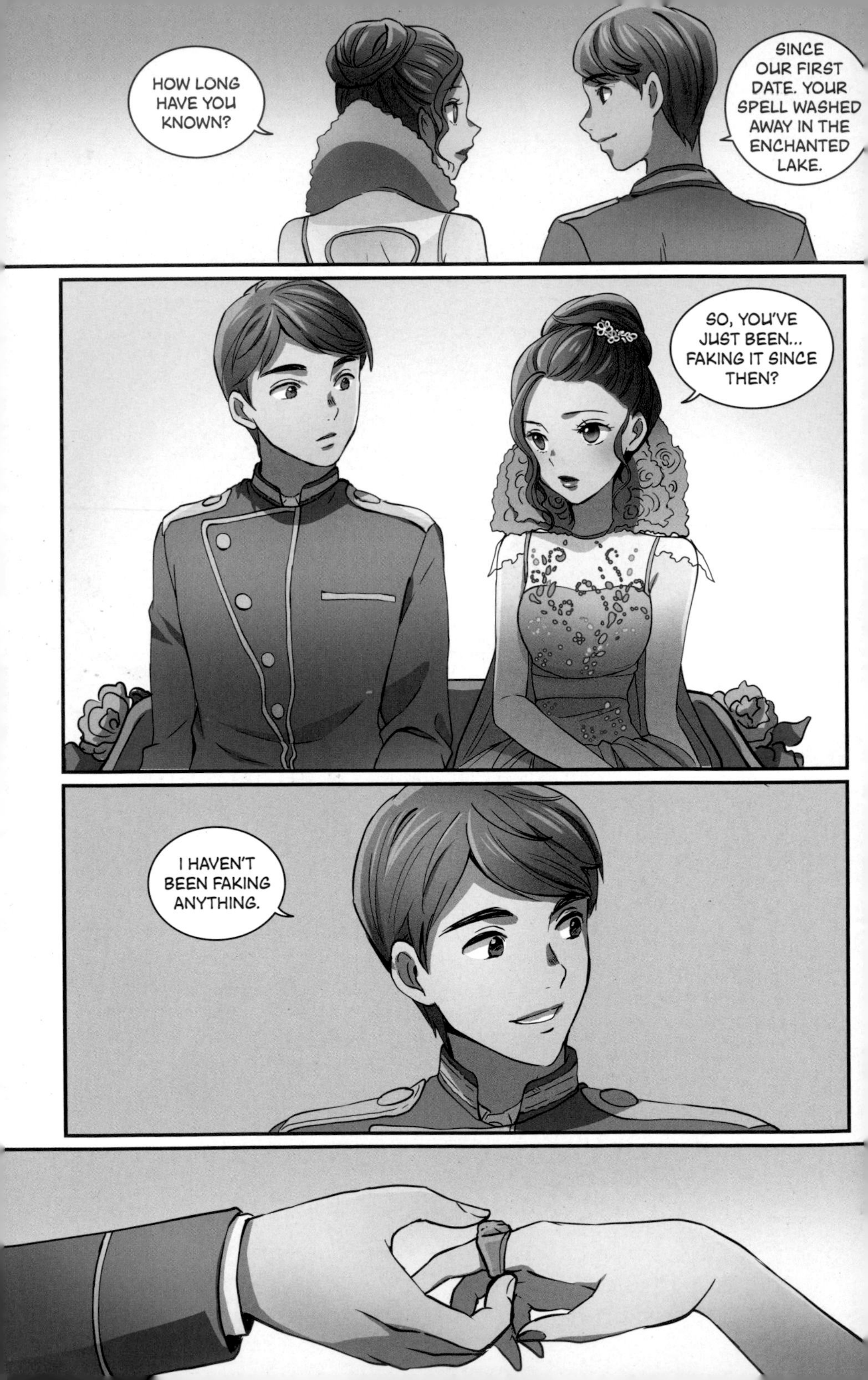
HOW LONG HAVE YOU KNOWN?
SINCE OUR FIRST DATE. YOUR SPELL WASHED AWAY IN THE ENCHANTED LAKE.
SO, YOU'VE JUST BEEN... FAKING IT SINCE THEN?
I HAVEN'T BEEN FAKING ANYTHING.

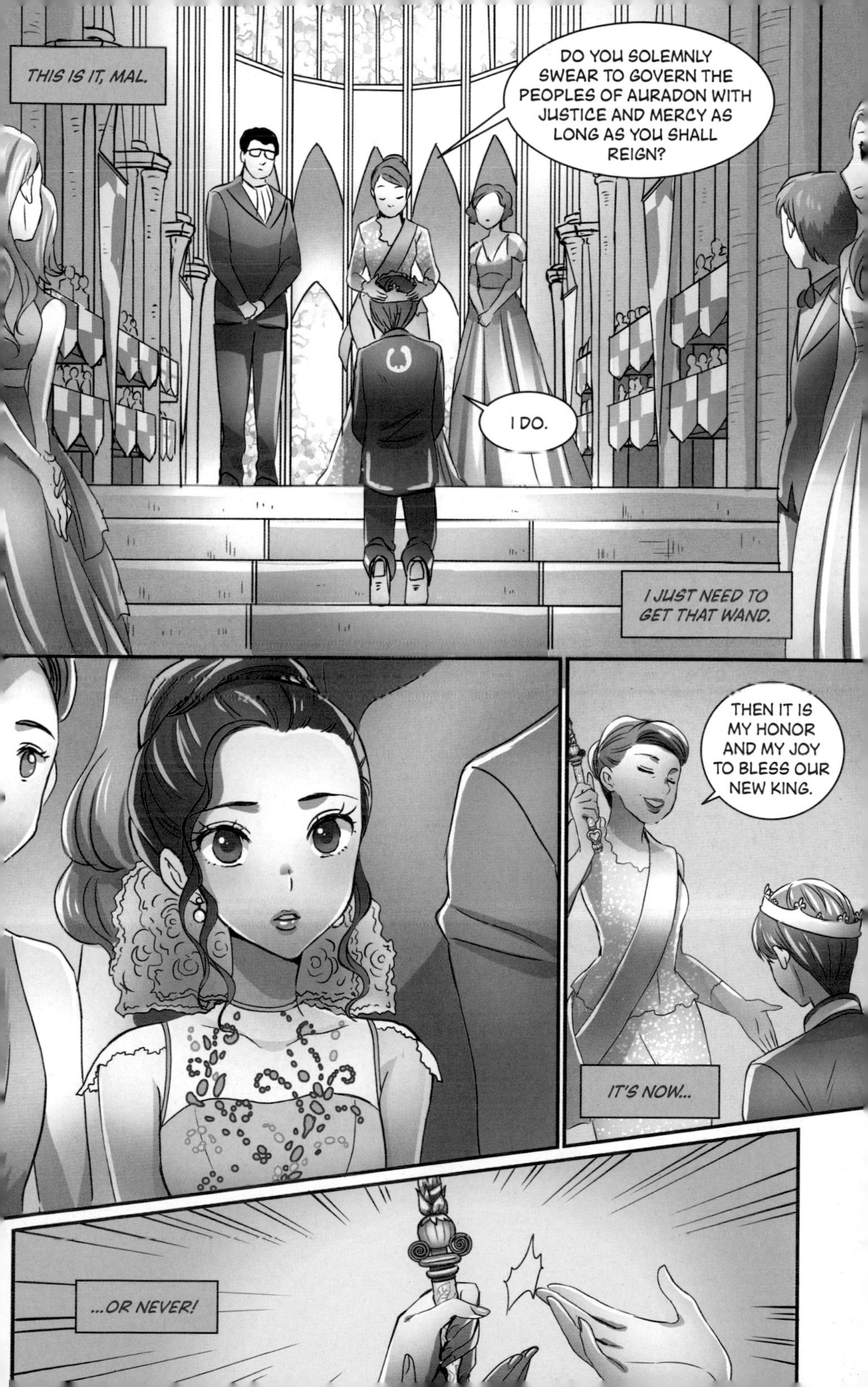
THIS IS IT, MAL.
DO YOU SOLEMNLY SWEAR TO GOVERN THE PEOPLES OF AURADON WITH JUSTICE AND MERCY AS LONG AS YOU SHALL REIGN?
I DO.
I JUST NEED TO GET THAT WAND.
THEN IT IS MY HONOR AND MY JOY TO BLESS OUR NEW KING.
IT'S NOW...
...OR NEVER!

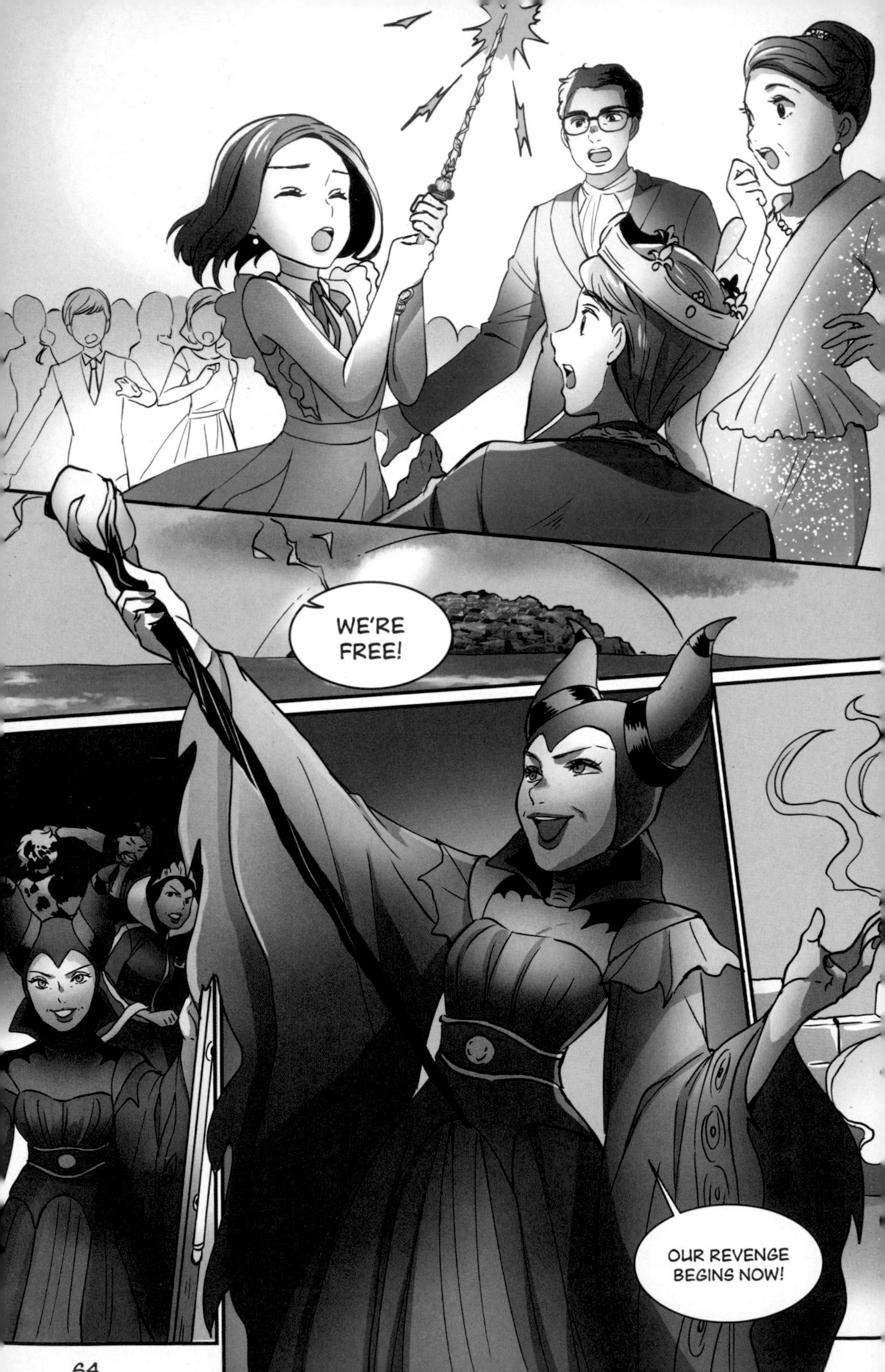
WE'RE FREE!
OUR REVENGE BEGINS NOW!

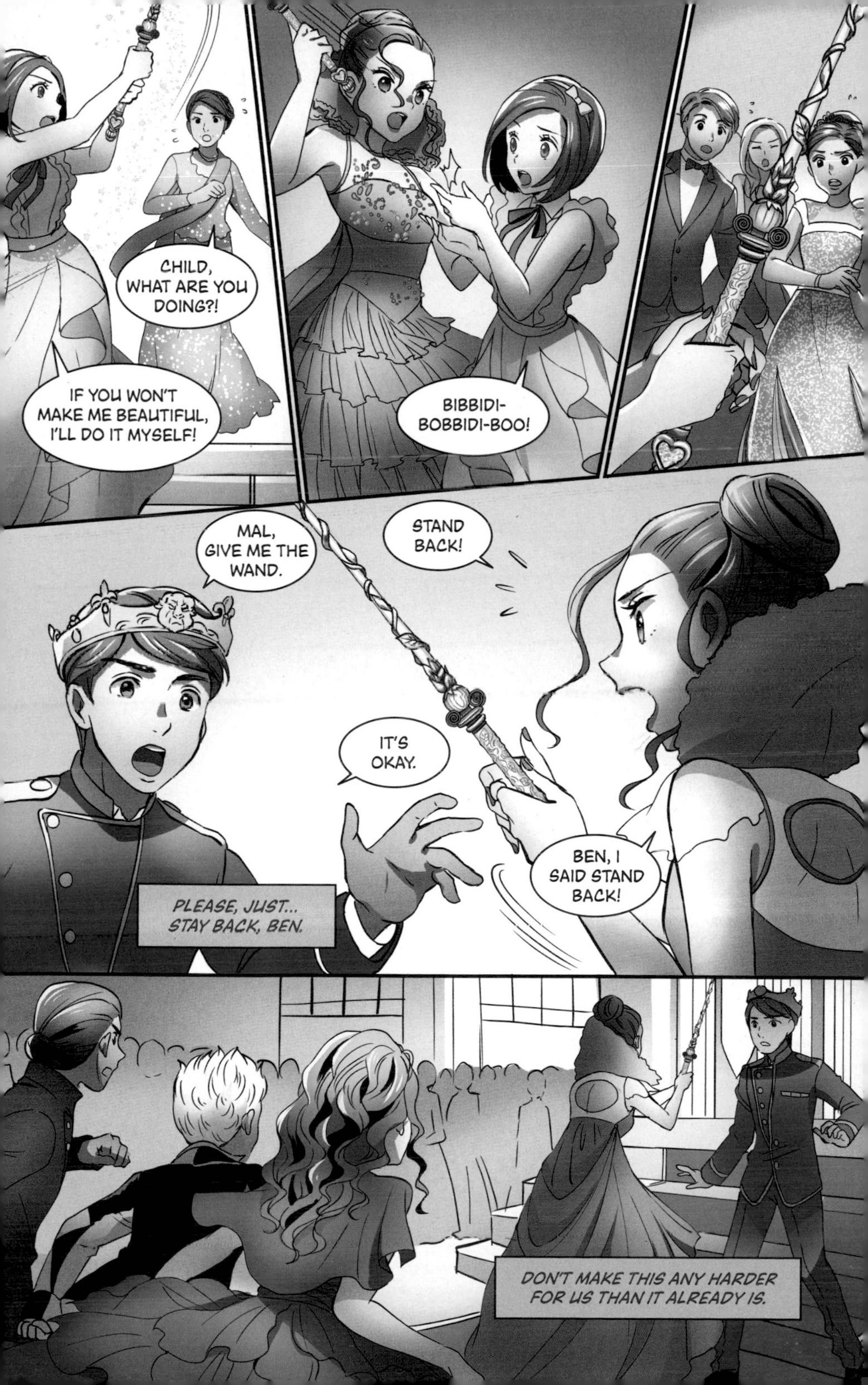
CHILD, WHAT ARE YOU DOING?!
IF YOU WON'T MAKE ME BEAUTIFUL, I'LL DO IT MYSELF!
BIBBIDI-BOBBIDI-BOO!
MAL, GIVE ME THE WAND.
STAND BACK!
IT'S OKAY.
BEN, I SAID STAND BACK!
PLEASE, JUST... STAY BACK, BEN.
DON'T MAKE THIS ANY HARDER FOR US THAN IT ALREADY IS.

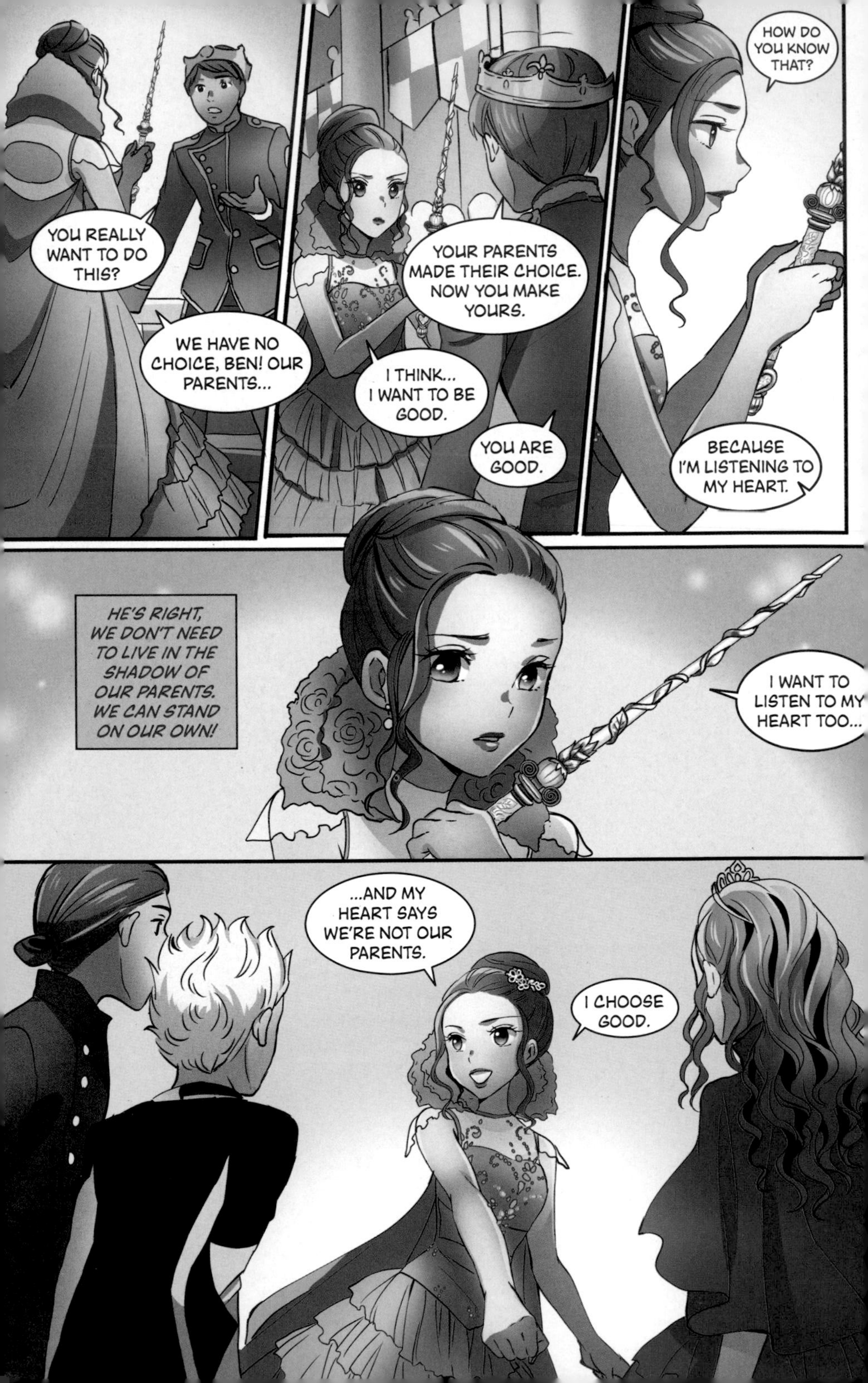
YOU REALLY WANT TO DO THIS?
WE HAVE NO CHOICE, BEN! OUR PARENTS...
YOUR PARENTS MADE THEIR CHOICE. NOW YOU MAKE YOURS.
I THINK... I WANT TO BE GOOD.
YOU ARE GOOD.
HOW DO YOU KNOW THAT?
BECAUSE I'M LISTENING TO MY HEART.
HE'S RIGHT, WE DON'T NEED TO LIVE IN THE SHADOW OF OUR PARENTS. WE CAN STAND ON OUR OWN!
I WANT TO LISTEN TO MY HEART TOO...
...AND MY HEART SAYS WE'RE NOT OUR PARENTS.
I CHOOSE GOOD.

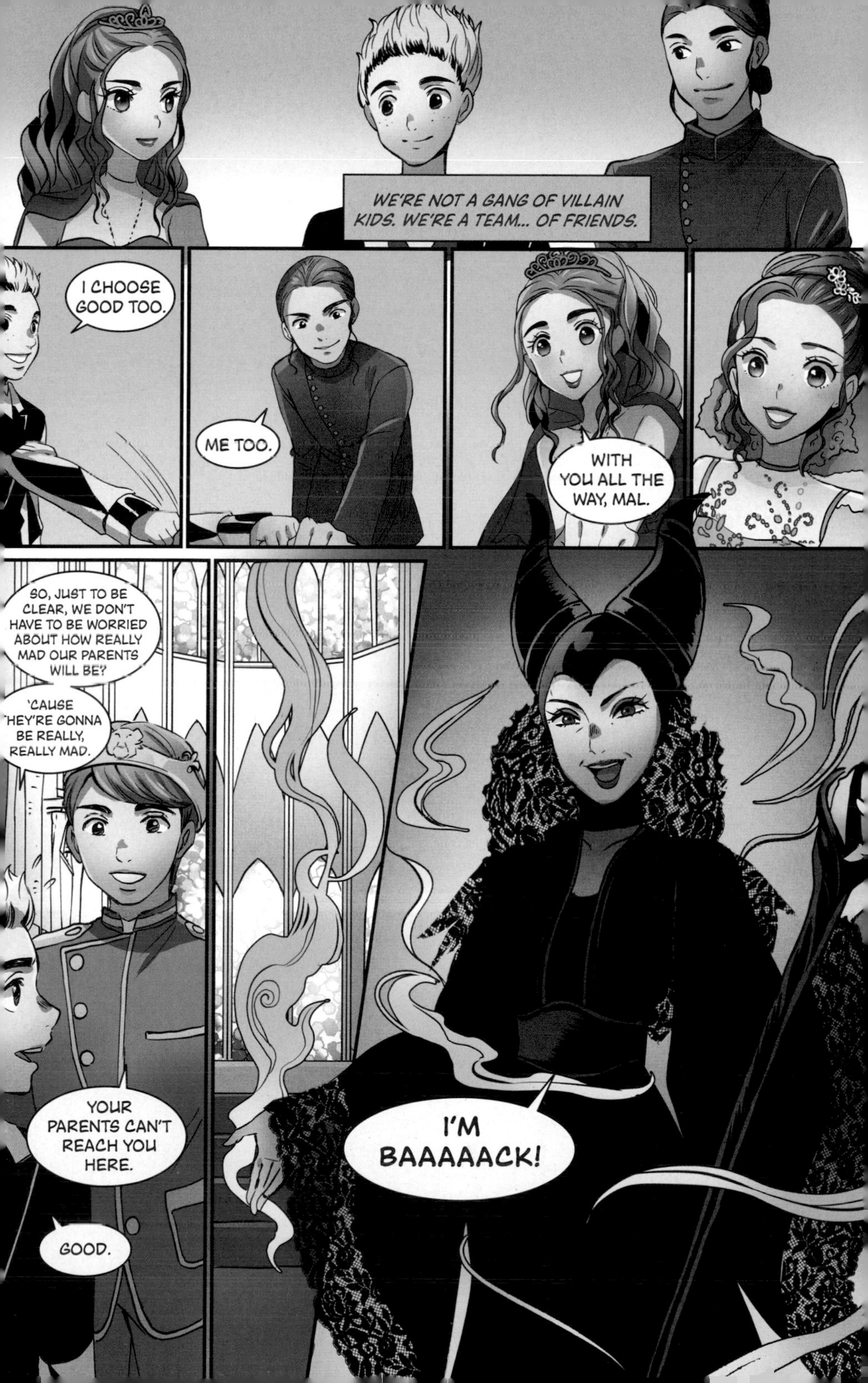
WE'RE NOT A GANG OF VILLAIN KIDS. WE'RE A TEAM... OF FRIENDS.
I CHOOSE GOOD TOO.
ME TOO.
WITH YOU ALL THE WAY, MAL.
SO, JUST TO BE CLEAR, WE DON'T HAVE TO BE WORRIED ABOUT HOW REALLY MAD OUR PARENTS WILL BE?
'CAUSE HEY'RE GONNA BE REALLY, REALLY MAD.
YOUR PARENTS CAN'T REACH YOU HERE.
GOOD.
I'M BAAAAACK!

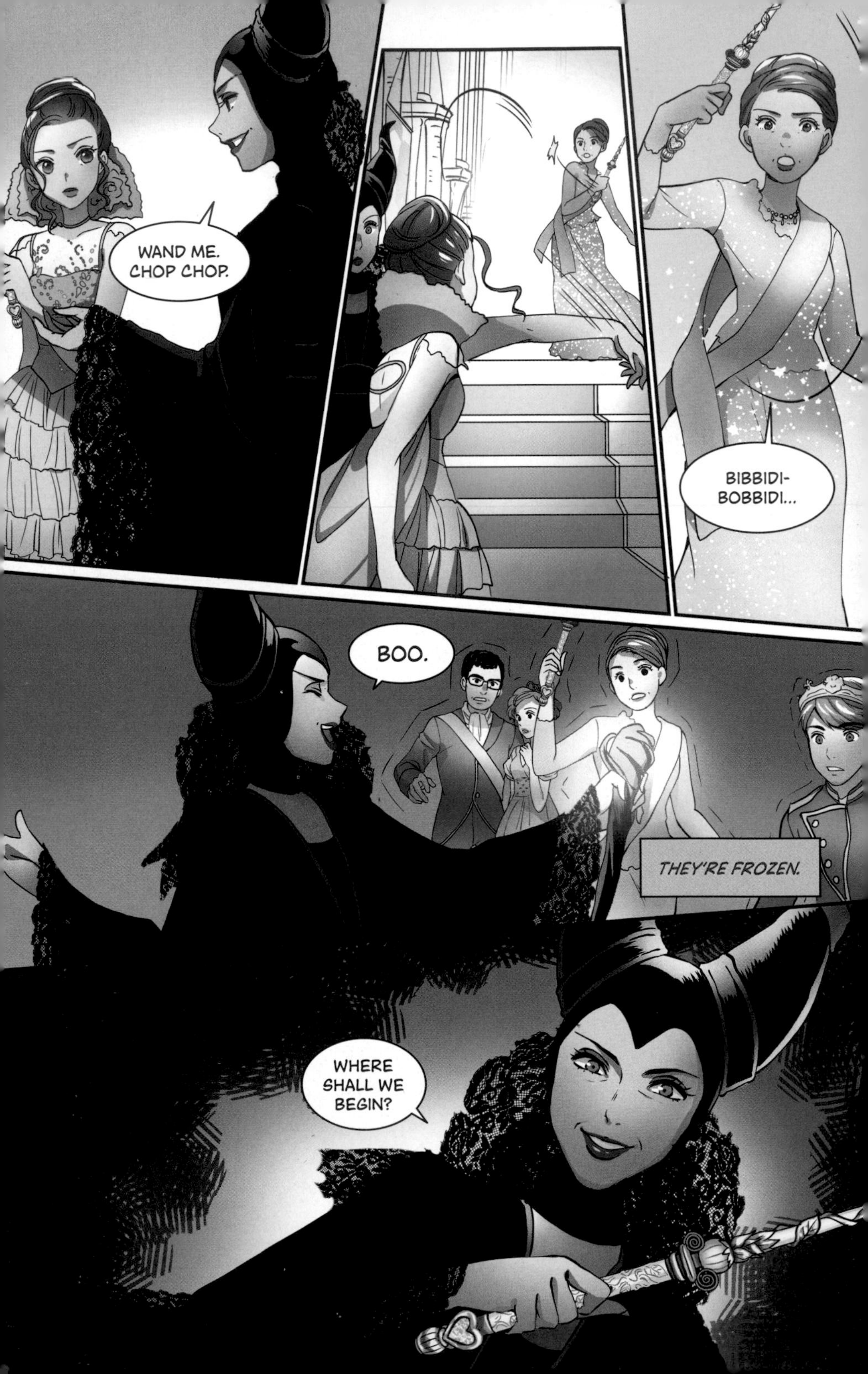
WAND ME. CHOP CHOP.
BIBBIDI-BOBBIDI...
BOO.
THEY'RE FROZEN.
WHERE SHALL WE BEGIN?

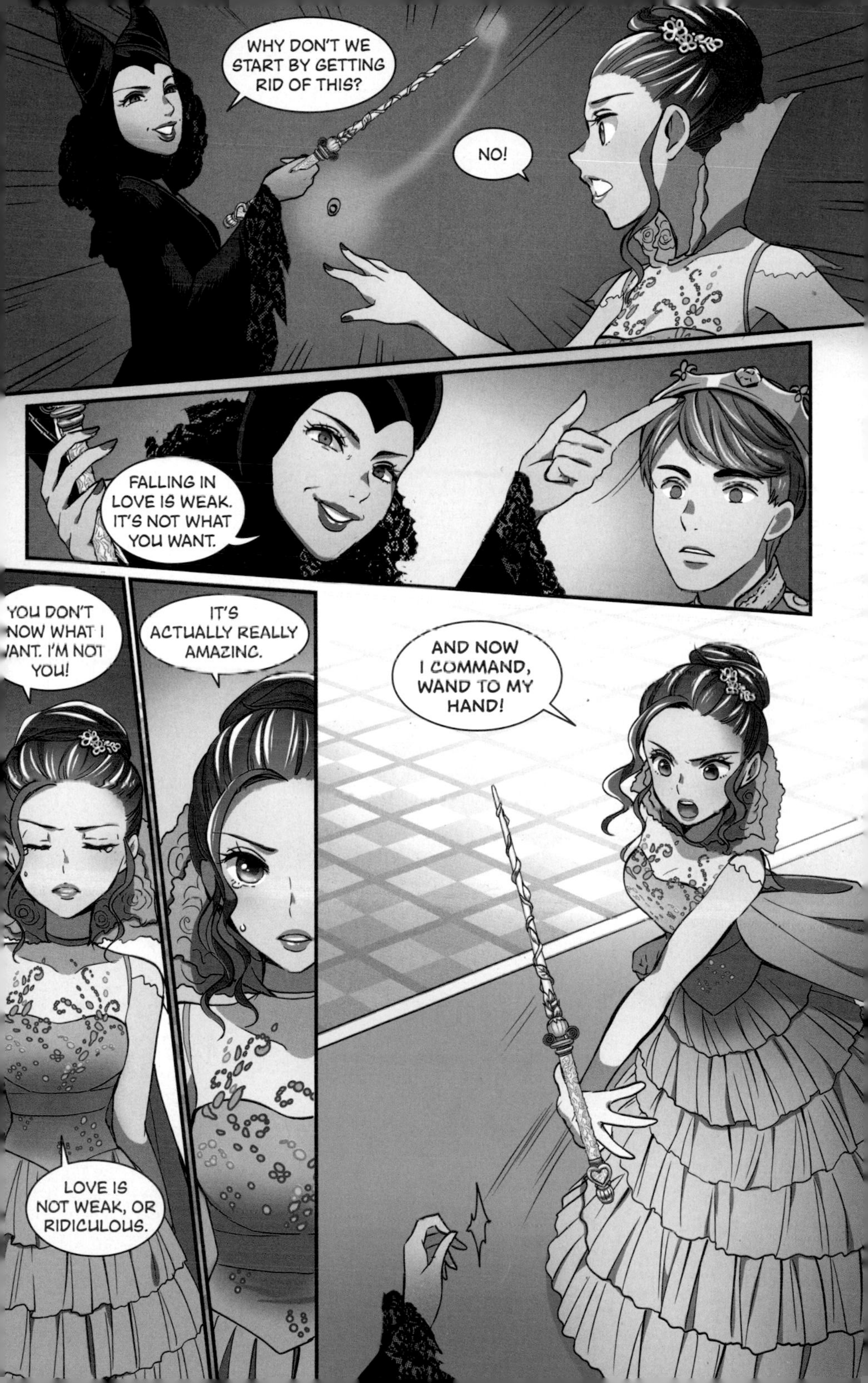
WHY DON'T WE START BY GETTING RID OF THIS?
NO!
FALLING IN LOVE IS WEAK. IT'S NOT WHAT YOU WANT.
YOU DON'T NOW WHAT I ANT. I'M NOT YOU!
LOVE IS NOT WEAK, OR RIDICULOUS.
IT'S ACTUALLY REALLY AMAZING.
AND NOW I COMMAND, WAND TO MY HAND!

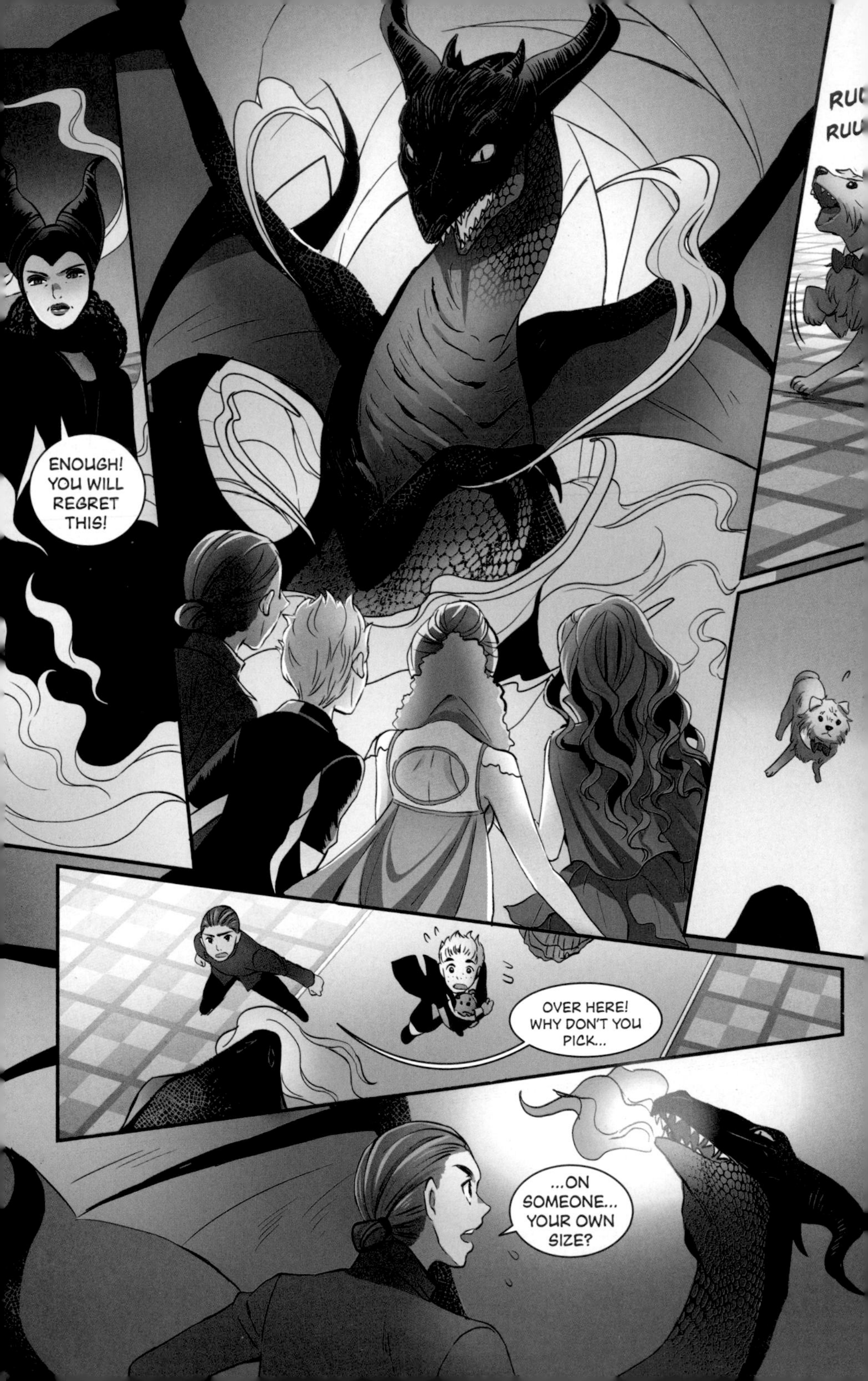
ENOUGH! YOU WILL REGRET THIS!
RUU
RUU
OVER HERE! WHY DON'T YOU PICK...
...ON SOMEONE... YOUR OWN SIZE?

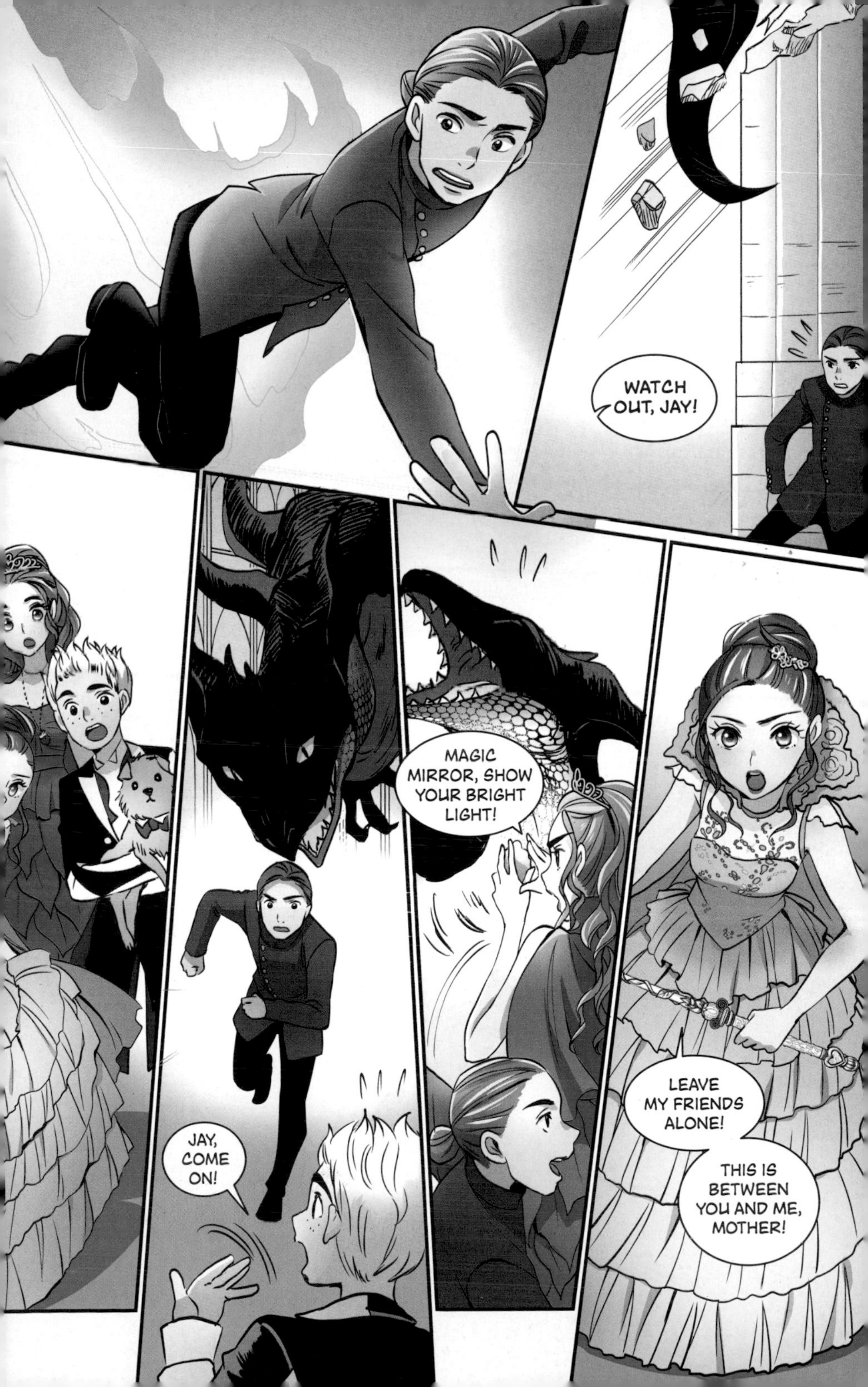
WATCH OUT, JAY!
LEAVE MY FRIENDS ALONE!
THIS IS BETWEEN YOU AND ME, MOTHER!
MAGIC MIRROR, SHOW YOUR BRIGHT LIGHT!
JAY, COME ON!

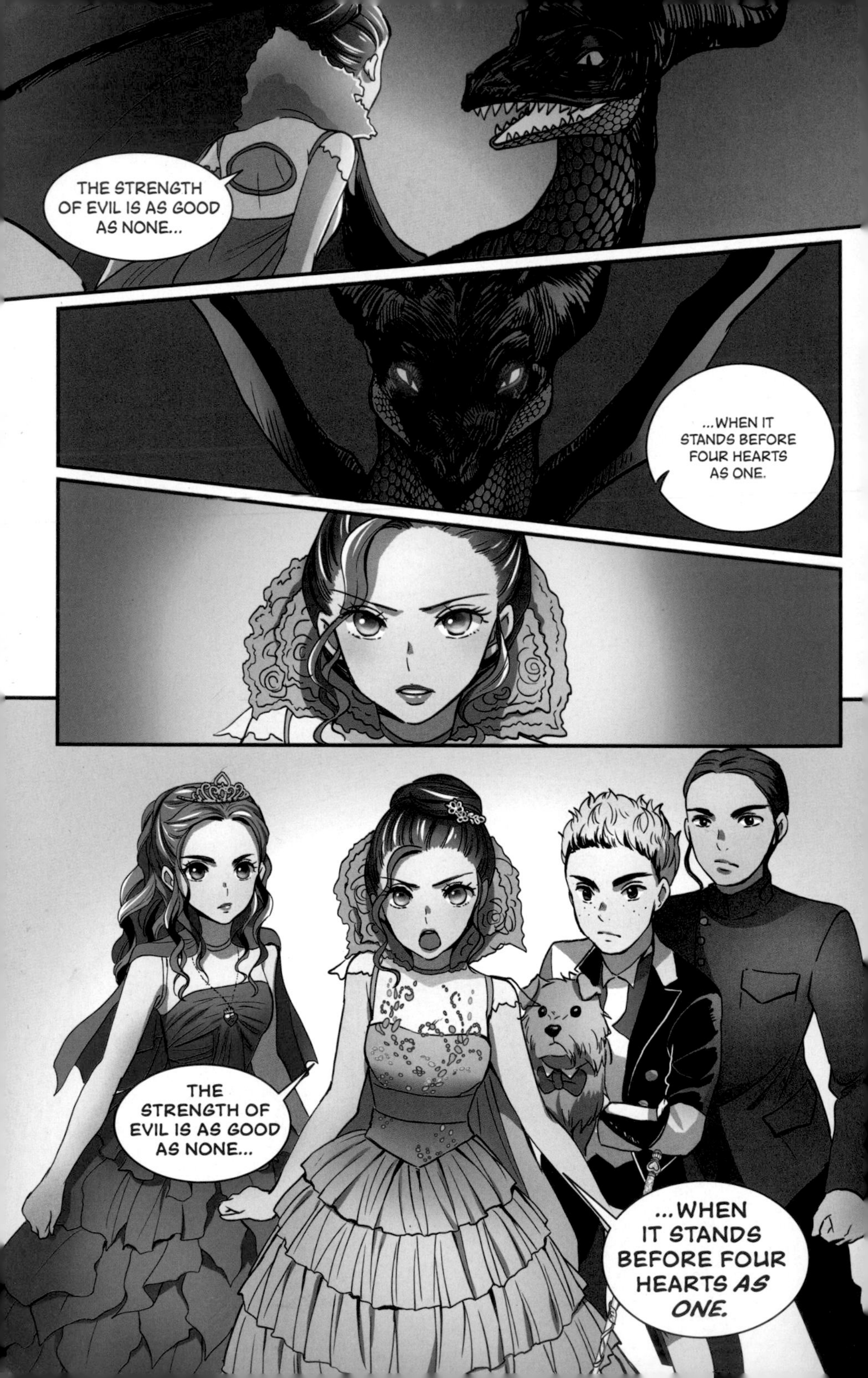
THE STRENGTH OF EVIL IS AS GOOD AS NONE...
...WHEN IT STANDS BEFORE FOUR HEARTS AS ONE.
THE STRENGTH OF EVIL IS AS GOOD AS NONE...
...WHEN IT STANDS BEFORE FOUR HEARTS *AS ONE.*

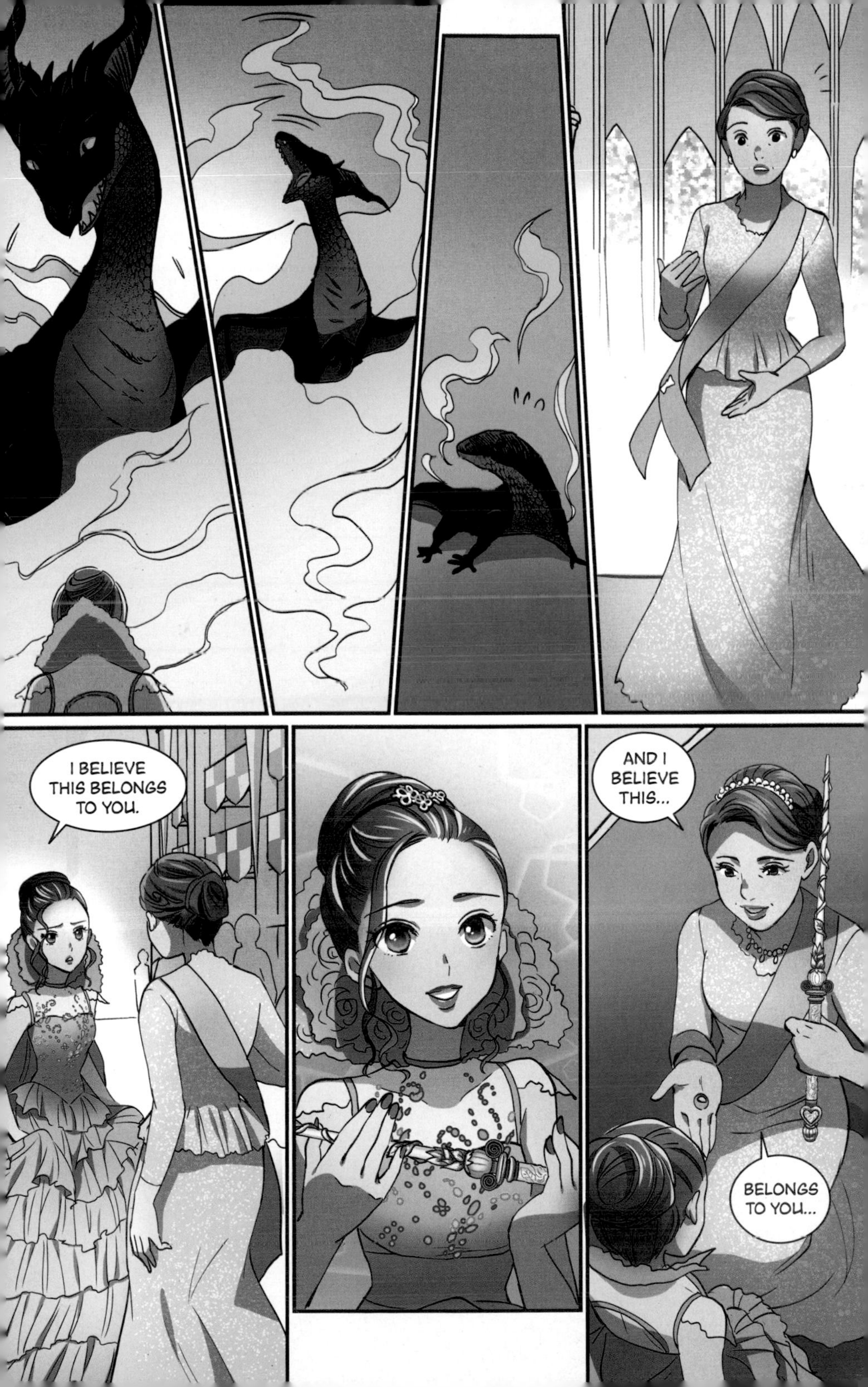
I BELIEVE THIS BELONGS TO YOU.
AND I BELIEVE THIS...
BELONGS TO YOU...

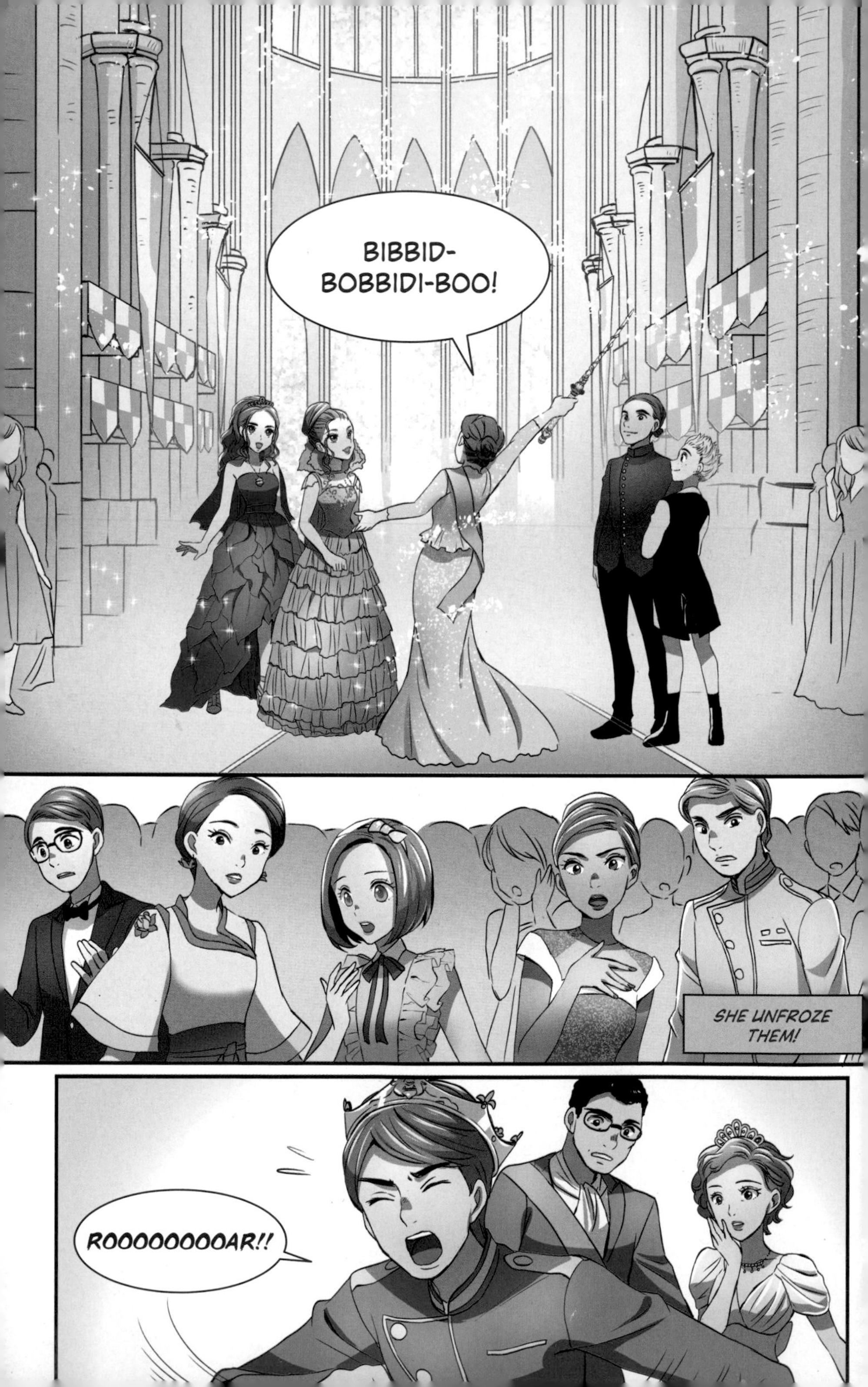
BIBBID-
BOBBIDI-BOO!
SHE UNFROZE THEM!
ROOOOOOOOAR!!

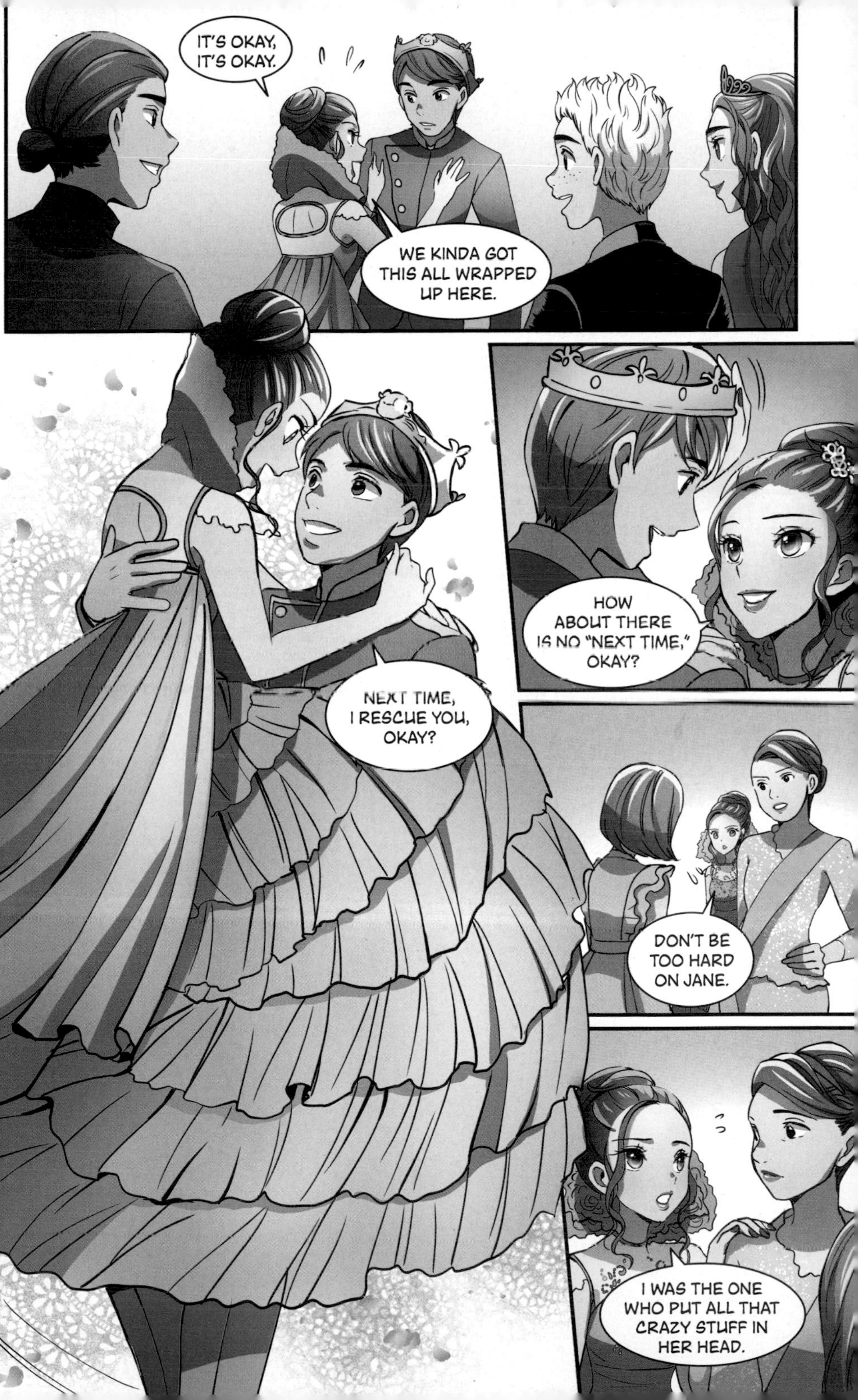
IT'S OKAY, IT'S OKAY.
WE KINDA GOT THIS ALL WRAPPED UP HERE.
NEXT TIME, I RESCUE YOU, OKAY?
HOW ABOUT THERE IS NO "NEXT TIME," OKAY?
DON'T BE TOO HARD ON JANE.
I WAS THE ONE WHO PUT ALL THAT CRAZY STUFF IN HER HEAD.

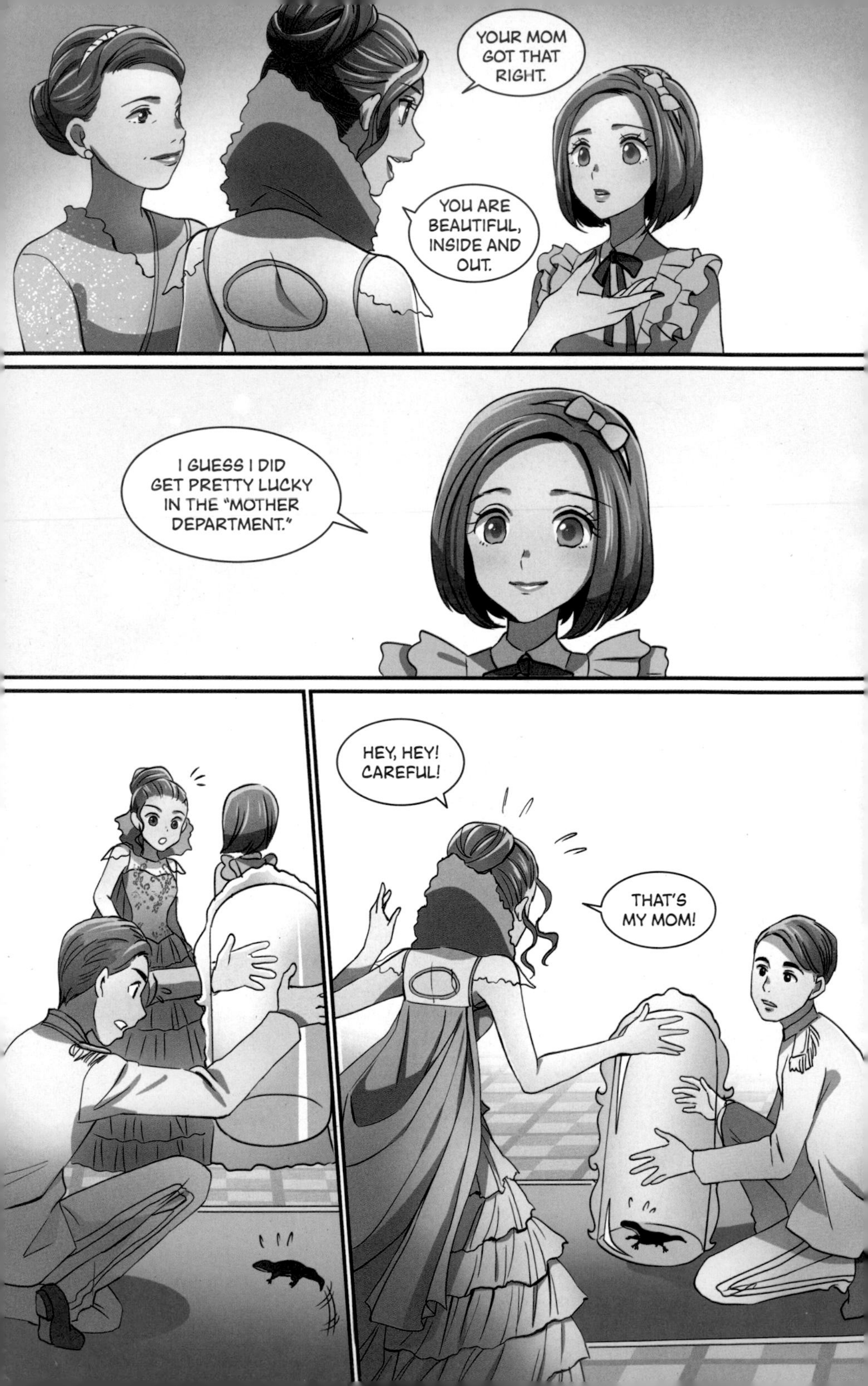
YOUR MOM GOT THAT RIGHT.
YOU ARE BEAUTIFUL, INSIDE AND OUT.
I GUESS I DID GET PRETTY LUCKY IN THE "MOTHER DEPARTMENT."
HEY, HEY! CAREFUL!
THAT'S MY MOM!

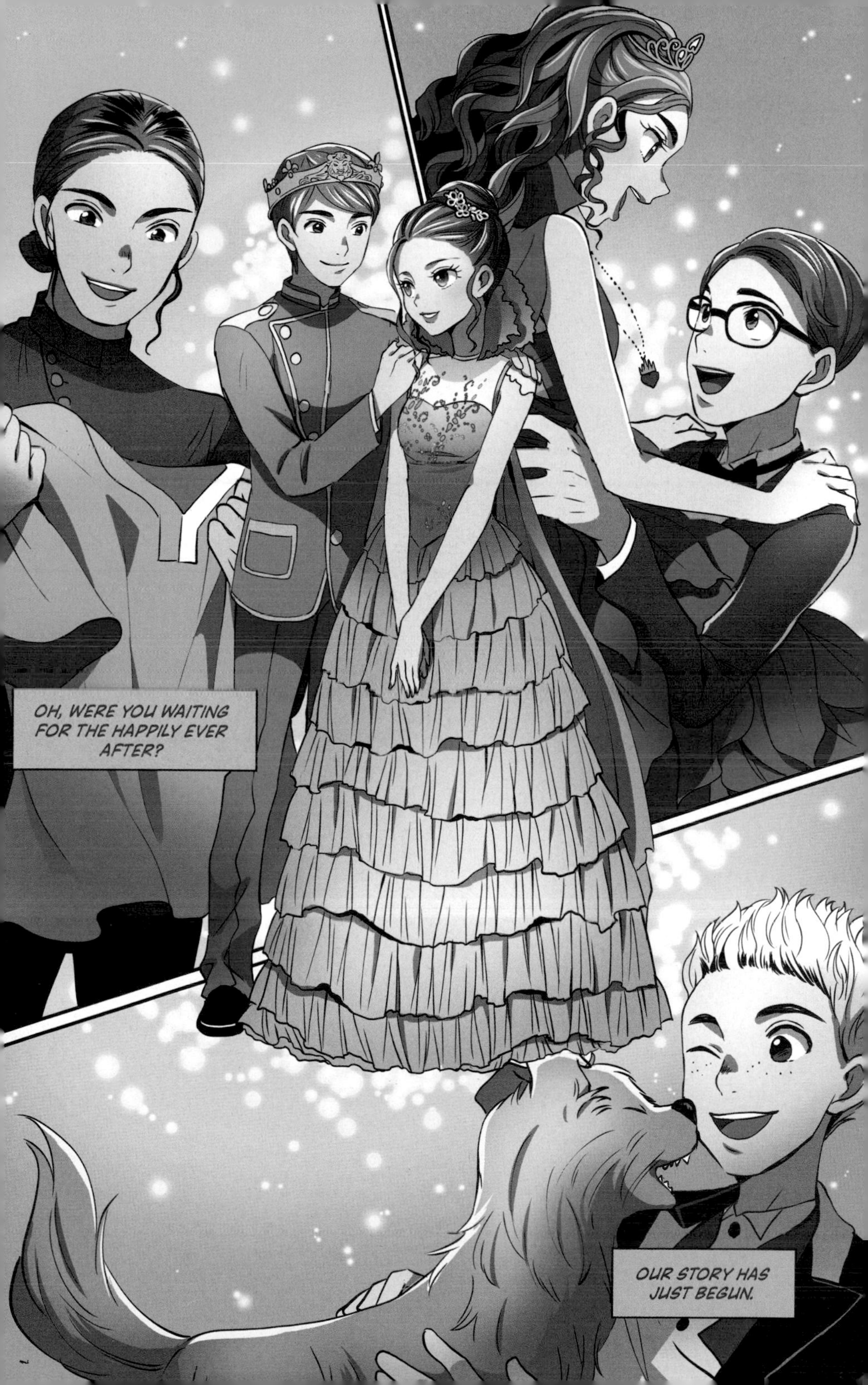
OH, WERE YOU WAITING FOR THE HAPPILY EVER AFTER?
OUR STORY HAS JUST BEGUN.

DID YOU ENJOY THE SERIES?

NEW STORIES COMING IN 2018!

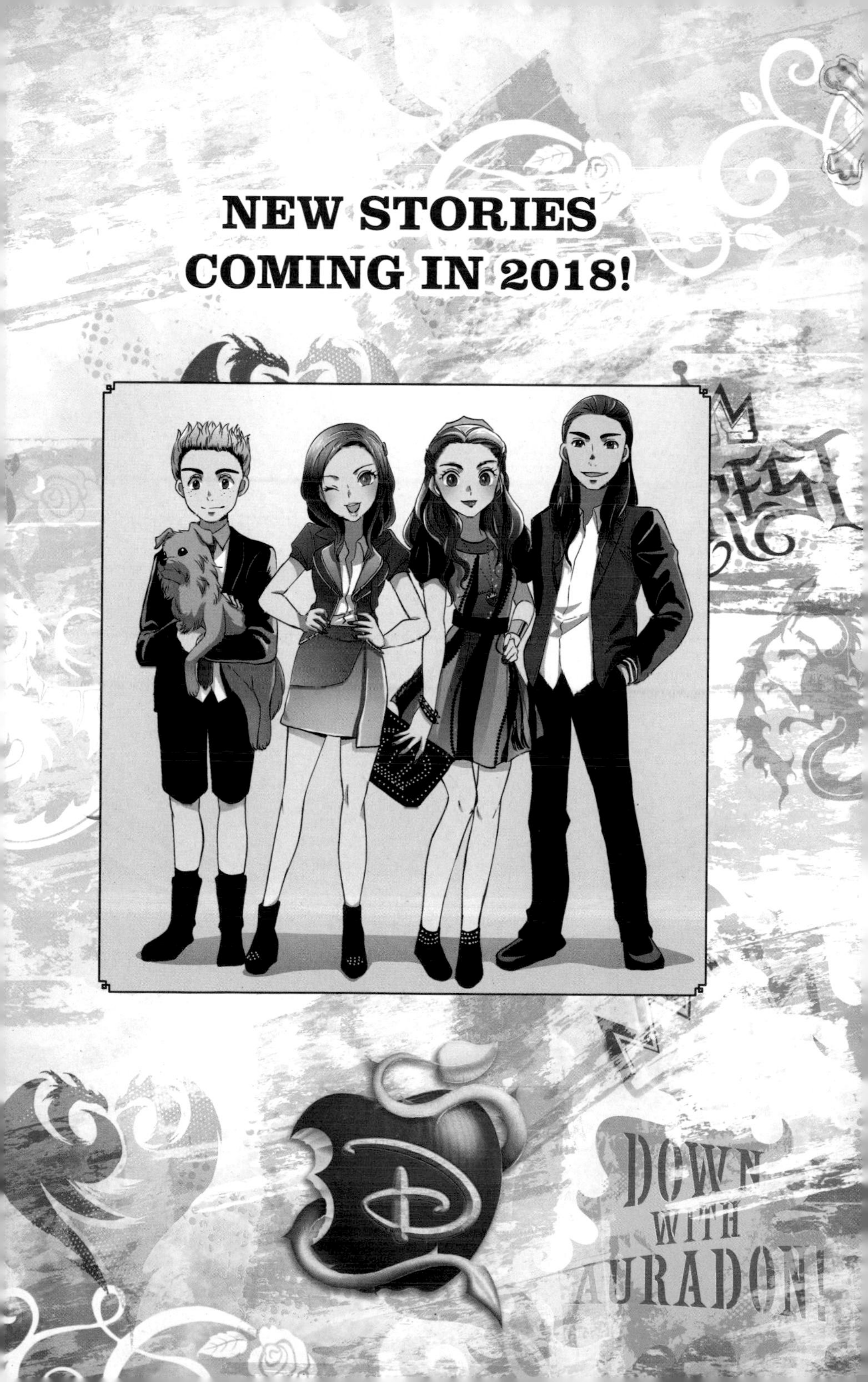

DOWN WITH AURADON!

Disney Descendants: The Rotten to the Core Trilogy Book 3
Art by : Natsuki Minami
Author : Jason Muell
Colorist : juryiaxreiria
Based on the hit Disney Channel original movie *Disney Descendants.*
Directed by : Kenny Ortega
Executive Produced by : Kenny Ortega and Wendy Japhet
Produced by : Tracey Jeffrey
Written by : Josann McGibbon & Sara Parriott

Publishing Assistant - Janae Young
Marketing Assistant - Kae Winters
Technology and Digital Media Assistant - Phillip Hong
Retouching and Lettering - Vibrraant Publishing Studio
Graphic Designer - Phillip Hong
Copy Editor - Daniella Orihuela-Gruber
Editor - Janae Young
Editor-in-Chief & Publisher - Stu Levy

A 🌏 **TOKYOPOP** Manga

TOKYOPOP and 🌏 are trademarks or registered trademarks of TOKYOPOP Inc.

TOKYOPOP Inc.
5200 W. Century Blvd. Suite 705
Los Angeles, 90045

E-mail: info@TOKYOPOP.com
Come visit us online at www.TOKYOPOP.com

f www.facebook.com/TOKYOPOP
www.twitter.com/TOKYOPOP
www.youtube.com/TOKYOPOPTV
www.pinterest.com/TOKYOPOP
www.instagram.com/TOKYOPOP
TOKYOPOP.tumblr.com

ISBN: 978-1-4278-5719-4
First TOKYOPOP Printing: October 2017
10 9 8 7 6 5 4 3 2 1
Printed in the CANADA